FILTHY PUCKBOY

RUSH HOCKEY #2

ELISE FABER

FILTHY PUCKBOY
BY ELISE FABER
Newsletter sign-up

This is a work of fiction. Names, places, characters, and events are fictitious in every regard. Any similarities to actual events and persons, living or dead, are purely coincidental. Any trademarks, service marks, product names, or named features are assumed to be the property of their respective owners, and are used only for reference. There is no implied endorsement if any of these terms are used. Except for review purposes, the reproduction of this book in whole or part, electronically or mechanically, constitutes a copyright violation.

FILTHY PUCKBOY
Copyright © 2022 Elise Faber
Hardcover Print ISBN: 978-1-63749-078-5
Print ISBN-13: 978-1-63749-077-8
Ebook ISBN-13:978-1-63749-076-1

RUSH HOCKEY

Big Puck Energy
Filthy Puckboy
So Pucking Over It

PROLOGUE

BAILEY

I'd dreamed of a two-towered bridge painted in International Orange.

I'd dreamed of fog crawling along the hill-filled city, creeping around skyscrapers, dancing over the rooftops of the Painted Ladies.

I'd dreamed of walking along twisting streets crowded with cars and of buying crabs fresh off the boat, steamed right there on the street corner, and made ready to eat with bare hands, delicious dunked in melted butter, napkins optional.

I'd dreamed of strong arms wrapped around me as we watched the sea lions bark on their platforms that floated alongside the pier, of sharing sourdough with a crust so thick that chewing it made my jaw hurt.

I'd dreamed of divvying up an ice cream sundae as big as my head, of music blaring out of club speakers, vibrating through our bodies melded together on the dance floor.

I'd dreamed of holding hands while riding the Ferris wheel in the park, my insides leaping and dipping as we rounded that big, *big* circle.

And more than anything, I'd dreamed of a sexy smile. *His* smile widening in surprise of me being there, of that surprise turning to excitement and joy and *heat*, his calloused hands trailing over my naked skin, of kisses and a hard cock and a night lost to lovemaking.

I'd dreamed of a man who could look at me and love me for me.

Of a man who looked at me and knew that I was enough.

A woman with small dreams and a quiet life.

A woman with heavy baggage and a prickly exterior.

A woman who was a little dinged and dented and...still enough.

But...dreams didn't come true.

God, I knew that.

I'd lived that enough in my twenty-five years to understand that my dreams didn't matter. Because every time I thought that my life was going to be different, that I was going to glide toward an ending that was happy and warm and everything my fantasies were made of, those dreams turned to nightmares.

One thread tugged and it all unraveled.

One wrong move and it all shattered.

One stuttered heartbeat and...I was broken.

ONE

BAILEY

Her nails dug into my arms tight enough to hurt.

She smelled like roses.

The familiar perfume was gentle and sweet.

But it didn't fit my mother.

Oh, her outside persona was all that was soft and womanly, with the feathers and fringe and loose, but perfectly draped clothing, the curls in her hair, the pale pink sparkles on her eyelids, the peach blush on her cheeks. But inside...*inside* she was a selfish snake who would go to any length to get what she wanted.

My mother should be in sky-high heels, a tight skirt, an equally fitted crisp white button-down, with red lipstick shining in the late afternoon sun. Heavy brows, fake lashes, tasteful and understated jewelry, hair slicked back into a fancy bun.

A shark in a businesswoman's clothing.

Instead...the woman standing in front of me was...what she was...

Awful.

And somehow, all of her femininity made it worse.

"My baby!"

It was loud and shrill, and I winced, pulling back, but that only made the nails dig in deeper. "Mom," I began, trying to pull back.

"I missed you so much!"

It was still loud and shrill...and it was a tactic to manipulate.

To distract me from the person, the *man* behind her.

Which I knew because those nails dug in, hard enough to leave deep indents on my skin, to send pain flaming through my arms, exactly like she used to do when I made her unhappy when I was a child and we were in public or with my grandparents, and she couldn't just smack the shit out of me like she did if we were alone.

Blond curls appeared in my periphery.

Billie Rose.

My aunt, who was closer in age to a sister, began to come near again.

And just as quickly the talons dropped away, my mother's face —and her fake smile—coming into view as she pulled back. Then she swung a hand in the direction of the house and my stomach began to churn. "The remodel is gorgeous!"

"The remodel." My voice was dead.

Because I already knew where this was going.

"Yes, honey." She laughed. "And I know you don't mind, but I moved your stuff into the guest room." A wink, like she was playing over-involved mother.

As if that had *ever* happened.

Under-involved was more like it.

Or only involved if it suited her or she got something from it.

Still, I braced, because I could already feel in my bones the next thing she was going to say. I already *knew* it.

"You and Colt can share," she stage-whispered.

I inhaled sharply.

So fiercely that I choked on the dust my truck had kicked up from the gravel and dirt road, and my throat spasmed in my effort to not bend over coughing.

I couldn't take my eyes off Colt.

It wasn't safe.

I stared at the man who'd left me with three broken ribs, a black eye, and running barefoot through the rain-filled night. A man I'd trusted with my heart and soul. A man I'd thought was my savior, my hope, my steady.

He wasn't.

He'd become...my nightmare.

But as I stared at him, I felt phantom fingers winding into my hair, gripping tight, yanking my head back. Felt those fingers clenched into fists colliding with my ribs, my stomach, my face. I could still feel the cold rain soaking into my clothes, my skin, chilling me, but not at much as the change the unraveling of my hope had rent on me.

That was when the numbness began to sink into my skin.

And...

I supposed I expected to feel real fear, coming face to face with my abuser.

He'd hurt me and left me with bruises and cuts and wounds that were far more than skin-deep. He'd lacerated my organs and soul and personality.

And...I didn't want to be that person again.

But...this day had been...

A lot.

Too much. My mind and senses were overwhelmed. I'd reached my limit before I'd even driven onto this scene.

So what I was feeling right at that moment was decidedly *numb*.

"You need to leave," I began—

Right as a car tore down the driveway, screeching to a halt behind me, kicking up more dust and sending my mom coughing, Billie Rose's expression turning into relief, and Colt skittering back, as though the dusty air might touch him and heaven forbid, he be contaminated by anything with the ranch.

That had been one of the final straws of our relationship—or maybe *the* final straw, if I was truly thinking about it, if I was actually putting the pieces of that demise together in my mind.

Gramps had asked me if I might be interested in moving closer, if I might help him and one day take over the ranch, and Colt...

Well, he hadn't liked that.

A car door slammed behind me, and I spun, heart squeezing hard when I saw Axel striding over to me. Relief, hurt, and worry rippled through me.

I'd driven four hours to get away from him, to run from the hurt that finding a naked woman in his hotel room had inflicted on me. I'd driven for four hours, sitting in the hurt, basking in it, wrapping it tightly around me...until it had turned to worry and I'd realized he wouldn't do that, realized I'd made a terrible mistake in running when I should have paused and just talked to him.

But by then I'd realized I'd lost my phone somewhere along the way.

I couldn't call him, couldn't talk things out.

But now...he was here.

And...his expression was a mix of too many emotions for me to decipher.

Then I didn't have a chance to because he was coming close, gripping my arms, but not how my mother had, not digging in, not hurting, not bruising and leaving marks.

"Buttercup—"

The morning came back.

The excited drive down. Knocking on his hotel room door.

The naked woman inside—

The lonely, heavy drive back.

And now this scene in my driveway, my parents, Colt, Billie Rose, and Axel...*Axel.*

Bad boy hockey player with the soft heart beneath. Former AHLer and now current San Francisco Gold starting forward. He'd made it to the big leagues. His hard work had paid off, finally, and even now, even after I'd driven home, spending almost four hours convincing myself that he might want to move on and it was better to let him go, I knew I couldn't. Mostly because after I'd realized I'd made a mistake, had reacted without thinking, I'd *then* spent the rest of the drive reminding myself that letting him go was a stupid thought because we'd pretty much crocodile death-rolled ourselves away from forming a relationship, but had still fallen and done it deep and...

He knew more about me than *anyone,* and I trusted him, and he was pretty much the best man I'd ever met and...

I didn't want him to let go, didn't want to be the one to disconnect.

Not without at least talking to him first.

I-I couldn't do that.

So that was why I covered his hands with mine and whispered, "Colt's here."

His fingers convulsed, but still not tight enough to cause pain. "The fucker who hurt you?"

"Yeah," I whispered.

He knew about Colt, but he didn't know *everything* about Colt, and I knew we had a lot to unpack there, too. But...later. Because I'd driven eight hours that day and half of them had been spent crying (or yelling) and the other half had been filled with hope and joy and *all* my dreams. I just didn't have much more emotion in me.

His eyes flicked over my shoulder then he bent closer. "And your parents?"

"Yeah," I whispered again.

"Fuck," he whispered back.

We had a lot to unpack there, too, but he knew enough to understand it wasn't a happy reunion.

Hell, we had a lot to unpack *everywhere*—from the naked woman in his hotel room to the shitstorm that was my past being here right in this moment.

But right then, all I wanted to do was step closer, to feel his arms wrap around me, to soak in his warmth and strength and—

Fuck it. I was going to do just that.

Forget the disaster waiting behind me.

Forget the turmoil that had prompted me to drive four hours with tears streaming down my face.

Forget everything but the way this man made me feel.

I was going to focus on that.

I needed Axel's arms around me, and that was that. Stepping forward, I said, "Axel, I—"

"Baby—"

Axel's arms had begun to wrap around me, instinctively giving me that closeness I craved, that I needed, but it wasn't his velvet rasp giving me the endearment.

It was Colt's gruff, cold voice.

Two

"Baby—"

My head shot up.

The fucker was staring at us unhappily, like I was encroaching on his territory by holding Bailey. He'd relinquished any claim the moment he'd hurt her, when he'd left her with trauma that had her flinching from my touch in the middle of the street, running from me when I would never *ever* lay a hand on her in anger, never intentionally hurt her.

But this man had.

And just that quickly, with only one thought, my anger was a dangerous thing.

Welling up like a storm gathering strength off the coast, getting ready to move slowly on shore, getting ready to wreak devastation in its path.

The fucker deserved a fist in the jaw, deserved *to have every bone in his body broken*.

But Bailey needed me more at that moment.

"No," I snapped when *Colt*—and what a stupid ass name the man had—came closer.

Bailey jerked in my arms when I spoke, but I just held on to her tighter. We weren't doing this. That fucker wasn't getting any closer to the woman I fucking *loved*, wasn't going to hurt her again. Not *ever* again.

"No," I repeated, sliding her to my side, tucking her close. "Stop *fucking* moving," I growled when it looked like her ex was going to reach forward and snatch her away from me.

Not that he would succeed in that.

But I didn't even want him breathing her air, let alone within five feet of her.

I was big. I was broad. I could take a hit and a punch or a puck to the fucking balls and keep on going. I could kill him, and wouldn't hesitate if Bailey's life was in danger.

This fucker knew it.

Because he stopped, though his expression made it clear he wasn't happy that I was still touching Bailey.

There was possession in the other man's expression, and plenty of it.

And *I* knew it, could identify it easily.

Because I felt the same way about this woman.

I *needed* to possess her, mark her, to make her mine in every single sense of the word.

The only difference was that I wouldn't hurt her.

Except, I could see the swelling around her eyes, the way the ends of her lashes were clinging together. She'd been crying. Because of me. Because of fucking *Candi* in my hotel room. Because Bailey had been there, too and she'd seen something that had sent her flying home...flying away from me. Away from me and into this fucking mess.

Away from me and onto a collision course with her ex.

Christ.

And her parents.

Fucking losers from what I knew, neglecting her, dragging her all over the Bay Area, running this place into the ground and then flitting off, leaving her to pick up the pieces.

Now the pieces had been picked up, had been fitted back into place.

And shocker of shockers, they'd "randomly" shown up.

"Who's this?"

A silken, feminine voice from the woman who looked like Bailey, but wrong. Too many feathers. Too much fringe. A hint of cleavage in a way that I knew was deliberate, would be wielded as a weapon at the first opportunity. I'd seen that predatory look on many women's faces.

"Axel," I said, not bothering to extend my hand.

I was an asshole.

That was my default position with most everyone.

River's Bend had somehow managed to get under my skin, Bailey even more deeply, so maybe I wasn't quite as much of a jerk with these people as I was with the rest of humanity, but I wasn't going to waste any of my limited niceness on this woman, on these fuckers.

"Baby—"

My gaze jerked to the side, to *Colt, who'd decided for some asinine reason, to speak again.*

God. What a fucking stupid name.

What a fucking stupid man if he thought that I was going to let him get any closer to Bailey.

"You moved my stuff into the guest room." Bailey's words were faltering at first, shaking before they steadied. She wasn't looking at Colt, hadn't acknowledged him in any way. Instead, her gaze was glued to her mother's. "You moved my stuff into the guest room so that I could stay with *him*—"

Now they were shaking again.

But not from fear.

From fury.

"You moved my stuff from *my* room," she snapped. "From the room I worked my *ass* off to save so this entire place didn't end up as some fucking development—"

"Language, Bailey."

A sharp whip of sound.

But not from her mother.

From the *fucker* with the stupid name.

From *Colt*.

And the effect it had on Bailey was instantaneous...and I fucking hated it. She jumped, burrowing against me, fingers tightening and they buried themselves in the fabric of my shirt.

I was going to kill this fucker.

But nearly as quickly as she'd tightened her grip, she released a breath, and I felt her forcing herself to calm, to steady, to straighten and pull slightly away from me.

The last, I hated.

I *got* it, understood why she did it, and I was fucking proud of her when she lifted her chin and whispered, "I will fucking talk however the *fuck* I want."

My fingers tightened on her waist.

"Now," she said, voice growing stronger. "I want you to leave." A beat. "*All* of you."

Her mother's face went from soft and sweet to sharp in an instant, and I knew, *knew* that my previous thoughts about her being predatory weren't unfounded. The woman might be the most dangerous person here.

Though the father hadn't spoken.

He might not be a *total* fucking useless sack of shit, standing there, doing nothing to protect his daughter, and surprise me...by being even more of a threat than the two assholes in front of us. But...life goals and all that.

Because at the moment, he had about as much use as one of Bailey's cows.

Less, I supposed, since we couldn't sell him for profit.

"Honey..." Bailey's mother began.

I turned away from her and the load of bullshit she was about to start spinning, gently cupping Bailey's jaw and tilted her head up so that her eyes hit mine. "Buttercup."

A shudder through her frame.

"I'm okay."

"I know." I ran my fingers gently over her skin, over the red around her eyes, gently across the damp lashes, separating them. "It'll be okay."

A tendril of fear in her chocolate brown eyes. "This is—"

"Breathe," I said when she broke off. "I'm here. We'll handle it together."

Another shudder, but this one wasn't from fear. It was relief, and fuck if that didn't settle into my heart.

I ran my thumb over her bottom lip. "Breathe, honey."

Honey because I wasn't ever going to call her baby again.

Because that motherfucker and the icy cold endearment that prickled along my skin, that disquieted my soul, wasn't going to be in our relationship. Not in a small way. Not in a big one. Not in *any* fucking way.

Her lips parted. Her breath slid out.

And then she inhaled. Exhaled.

Once that was steady, I tucked her close again, turned to the trio of assholes, "She asked you to leave."

"My stuff—" her mother began.

"Right here," Billie Rose said cheerfully, bursting in a little breathlessly, as though she'd been running around. And maybe she had, considering that she dropping a turquoise bag onto the gravel just in front of Bailey's mother's feet. Several more soon joined the others—though they weren't suede, just a mix of plastic-sided suitcases and a couple of plain duffles. "Don't worry if I forgot something," Billie added sunnily. "I'm happy to drop it by where you're staying." A beat, all warmth having left her tone. "Which is, hopefully, not in River's Bend."

I had the feeling that even if they tried to stay at the B&B in town or the hotel that bordered River's Bend but was technically the next town over, they would find all the rooms had been filled up.

Thus was the power of Billie Rose.

The mayor of River's Bend had her fingers in everything.

Couldn't stop these fuckers from showing up on Bailey's doorstep though.

Couldn't stop *Colt* from hurting her.

Couldn't stop—

"My bag!" It was a screech as Bailey's mother lurched forward and picked up the suede tote from the ground, clutching it to her chest like it was a baby who had just bonked her head. She began frantically dusting it off, trying to remove every last speck of dirt. "How dare—"

"She asked you to leave," I said.

"And I've already called Frank. That's the sheriff," Billie Rose added in a stage whisper. "In case you've forgotten."

Bailey's mother hissed out an annoyed breath.

"Also, since I know that none of your names are on the deed or the mortgage"—another annoyed breath—"I don't think he'll take kindly to you three trespassing..."

She trailed off.

The silence stretched.

And stretched.

Until Billie Rose glanced behind them, eyes narrowing as she presumably focused on some spot in the distance. "Ah, yes, I see that he's coming right now."

Thankfully, that was the impetus to get the fuckers moving.

The bags made it into their rental car.

The people—Colt with another glare at me—climbing into the driver's seat.

A fact I noted.

A fact I really didn't like.

But then the doors were closed, and they were skidding out of the driveway, kicking up rocks and dirt and dust.

I turned to Bailey, opened my mouth,

And didn't get one word out before Billie Rose snagged her arm and dragged Bailey away from me.

THREE

Billie Rose's grip was tight too.

But it didn't hurt either.

I sucked in a breath, released it slowly as the truth of that hit home.

And if anything, it settled me further, allowed the tightness gripping my lungs to loosen.

"What happened?" Billie asked once we were five feet away from Axel.

As though that would stop him from listening. He wasn't a good guy—okay, so he was the *best* guy—but he didn't have pesky things like...morals.

At least when it came to eavesdropping about things that concerned me.

He...was protective.

He was mine.

And if the shit that had just gone down in my life had gone down in front of me in *his*, then I'd be playing starfish, clinging to a rock nearby and doing everything to make sure he was okay.

Bad analogy.

Still the truth.

Which was why I glanced over my shoulder and caught his gaze.

His eyes were gentle, though his face was still set in hardened lines that were so sharp they threatened to cut. I wanted to shrug off my aunt's hold, wanted to walk right back into his embrace, to wrap my arms around him and make that hard and sharp go away. But then Billie Rose tugged at my arm, and I pulled my stare from the pretty, pretty man behind me and focused.

"Are you okay?" Billie asked.

I laughed.

Because I was pretty much as far from okay as I could be.

"You mean because I drove four hours to surprise my boyfriend, only to knock on his hotel room door and have it opened by a naked woman who said he'd brought her there?" I laughed, and yeah, it was slightly hysterical. "But she was gracious and offered to let me stay around because he prefers fucking two chicks at once, so at least I've got that going for me."

I heard a growl, saw the lines of his face grow even harder.

I softened my tone. "And maybe I could have discounted it outright because she was giving all sorts of crazy, stalker woman vibes, but then she described my boyfriend's tattoo and the scar just above his right hip and—"

That growl grew louder, and I felt Axel move closer.

"And then after driving almost four hours back home thinking I'd made a huge, huge mistake in letting that man into my life and not recognizing until I was nearly home that I hadn't actually talked to him and that I probably should..." I sighed and Billie's face gentled. "But it was then that I realized I'd left my cell in the hotel room with the naked woman so I couldn't actually call him." I shook my head. "But *then* I drove right onto a scene where my estranged parents had moved my belongings into my guest room so I could share with my ex who beat the shit out of me, leaving me with broken ribs, a concussion, and shredded feet."

Billie's hand convulsed, her face no longer anywhere near gentle.

"*What?*" Axel's voice rose. "I'm going to *kill* that motherfucker."

Right.

I needed to prioritize here.

Tugging free of my aunt, I spun back to face him.

Yup. All sharp lines and fury having burned away any glimmer of soft.

"It's okay—" I began.

"*It's not fucking okay.*"

A burst of sound, guttural and fierce and sounding as though it had been torn from him.

"I meant," I said, walking toward him, my heart squeezing tight when his arms immediately opened and he welcomed my body against his, "*I'm* okay. What he did wasn't and never will be, but...*I'm* okay and I-I don't want to go back there, okay? I just want to be here with you and—"

Naked woman in his hotel room.

He must have seen that thought—or maybe the insecurity—flit through my mind, because immediately his face softened, and he cupped my cheek. "We need to talk," he whispered.

"I know," I whispered.

"Buttercup—"

Rocks crunched behind us, and I turned to see Frank pulling into the driveway, his cruiser's lights off, but his speed urgent enough that I knew Billie Rose had lit a fire under his ass to get out here.

"For the record, even with all my fuckups, you didn't once threaten to call the sheriff on me," Axel said lightly, and I knew he'd both tempered his anger and set aside the soft.

At least for the moment.

Snark was back.

The arrogant, filthy puckboy who had a wall up between himself and the rest of the world was back.

That sent a curl of fear through my belly.

Then his thumb trailed over the inside of my wrist, a featherlight touch that told me...enough.

That the wall might come up around others, but that the wall didn't exist, not for me.

I took a breath, released it slowly, my eyes drifting to the dust cloud in the distance, the speck that was Colt and my parents' car growing smaller with each passing moment.

Billie Rose chuckled softly, and I glanced over in time to see her pat his arm. "I didn't need to pull out the big guns, honey bun," she said, grinning at Axel and then at me. It was a bit frayed at the edges, but it was there. Progress. Another pat to his arm. "You're harmless."

Somehow, despite everything, amusement bubbled in my chest at the notion of anyone calling the six-foot-plus, over two hundred pounds of muscled hockey player harmless, and the fact that I could feel *anything* except horror and anger and fear and fury was a fucking miracle.

But thus was the power of Billie Rose.

She backed up, turned toward Frank, who was now getting out of his cruiser. "Stop right there, Franklin Horst."

Frank stopped, eyes widening. "Um, what?"

"Back to the high school with you," she said. "The football fans won't police themselves."

"I—" He lifted a hand, gestured toward us, himself. "But you—"

"Back in the cruiser, Horst," Billie Rose ordered.

Another gesture. "I—"

"Shoo."

Frank's hand fell to his side. Then he shook his head, once, twice. *Then* he turned and walked back to his car, pulling the door open, getting in, and backing out of the driveway as quickly as he'd pulled in.

"Right," Billie Rose said, nodding sharply.

Axel stiffened next to me, and I braced.

"I've got things to do to prepare for the Winter Festival." She dragged the handle of her purse up her shoulder, clapped her hands together. "My spreadsheet is sorely out of date and..."

She didn't bother to finish the sentence.

Just turned and walked away from us.

And then her car joined the cruiser on the road, trailing dust and turning into a barely visible speck.

I glanced up at Axel.

He stared down at me.

I opened my mouth—

"There's a Winter Festival?"

FOUR

She was fucking beautiful in the fading sunlight.

Even more so when she smiled.

"Yeah," she whispered. "There's a Winter Festival and a Spring Festival. And Summer and one for Valentine's Day called Spread the Love, and a Bunny Hop, and—"

"Buttercup?"

She'd been ticking them off on her fingers, but at the nickname she stopped, looking back up at me. "Yeah—"

I didn't stop to think, didn't wait to consider.

We needed to talk. We needed to talk about so many things.

But the woman I loved was in my arms.

And I needed to taste her.

So, I did.

Just bent my neck and let my lips hit hers.

She melted, and I nearly did too as *right* surged through every cell in my body. Her lips were the softest thing I'd ever felt, and she smelled like an apple orchard, floral and fruity. Her body fit against mine, just fit in a way that was so *right* that it deserved poetry or some shit, but it was romantic shit that I never fully managed to grasp or verbalize and so I just had to settle for slipping my tongue between her lips and kissing the shit out of her.

Hands palming her curves.

Tongues tangling.

Mouths battling for dominance.

But she always let me win, and that had my cock going hard in an instant, remembering *all* the ways she'd let me win...even when she'd ended up on top.

But—

I tore my mouth from hers.

"Candi and I didn't—"

Her lips were swollen, eyes half-mast. But my words had the heat fading from those pretty chocolate brown irises, her expression going somber. "I know."

My brows dragged together. "Then why—"

"Did I leave?" she asked.

I nodded. That seemed to be the obvious question.

A half-smile curved her mouth. "It took me approximately three and a half hours to realize that I might have misinterpreted what went down with Candi. Like I mentioned before, she was... very specific about parts of your body and the things you did and..." A sigh. "I was hurt and ran...and by the time I realized that I needed to call you and get some answers, I was closer to home than San Francisco." She shrugged, her eyes asking for forgiveness. "And then I didn't have my phone. I'm sorry, honey. Sorry I scared you. I should have stopped and thought and—"

I touched her cheek. "Right. First." I dug into my pocket, pulled out her cell, and handed it to her.

"Thanks," she whispered, pocketing it.

"I showed up at the hotel room and I found it, along with—" I broke off, unsure how to phrase all that had gone down with Candi.

"A gorgeous naked woman with more than slightly crazy eyes?"

Of course she'd sum it up perfectly.

"Yeah," I whispered. "*That.*"

Teeth pressing into her bottom lip, her eyes locked on mine. "What happened?"

"You know Brit offered me her old apartment."

She nodded.

"I went over last night to check it out and bring some of my stuff. Then Brit and the guys showed up and we ended up having an impromptu game night, so I slept there." Her hair, that gorgeous silky brown hair that shone like the fucking sun, was in her eyes so I pushed it back, tucked a strand behind her ear. "Then in the morning I went back to change and grab the rest of my shit because I was going to come up and surprise you and—"

"Candi was there."

"Yeah. With an *i.*"

She froze.

And then she did the most wonderful thing ever. She *laughed*. "With an *i?*"

My lips twitched. "Yeah."

"Yikes." Another laugh, but this one was accompanied by warmth dancing through her eyes, amusement gilding her smile. "It's worse than I thought."

"Yeah." I tucked another strand of hair behind her ear. "Worse."

She went sober again and I watched the insecurity creeping back into her expression. Fuck. I hated that *I* was the cause of that hurt. That the pain in her eyes was because *I'd* caused it. "What did she say to you?"

White teeth into a plump bottom lip. "She was...very descriptive about you...and um...your tattoo."

I stilled.

"And..." A sigh. "Your scar. She was *very* detailed when talking about your scar."

Fuck.

Fuck.

I inhaled, released it slowly.

"I know that you...um...were with a lot of women before me." Her lips tipped up and her smile wasn't anything close to real, her stare tempered with pain. "Hell, I know I wasn't the town manwhore, but I was with enough people to know that I can't fault you for the same. It was before me"—she paused, eyes glinting with enough hesitation that I nodded, even though it fucking stung—"it was before me," she repeated.

"It was before you," I said, giving her the words because I *had* to, because she needed to know.

She needed *to know.*

She nodded again, the edges of her eyes warming.

"And I wasn't with her. Not *ever.*"

"Axel—"

"Not *ever*, buttercup," I said again. "I was with her friend. We finished and—" I winced, because, fuck, I was an asshole. But I pushed on and gave her the rest. "I looked up and Candi was standing there, watching me—" I broke off, shuddering.

Her fingers tightened on my chest, the warm growing, being joined with empathy. "Being creepy as fuck?" she whispered.

"Yeah." I took a breath and released it. "So that's how she would know about my scar, about my tattoo. She was watching, and apparently doing it for a while. But I swear I didn't—not with her—not—"

"I know."

Now her tone was steady, full of conviction, and finally, finally, I relaxed. "Yeah?"

A nod. "Yeah, honey."

My breath slid out of me, slow and steady. "Then want to tell me why we're still standing out here when we're finally together?"

"I—"

She froze and then her hand came to my jaw, rested there lightly, fingers stroking gently through my beard.

I shivered.

Fuck, I loved it when she did that.

It set my nerves on fire.

Then she smiled, fingers pressing in, the tips hitting my skin and sending need billowing through me. My cock was still hard from the kiss, from her body against mine, but when she smiled like that, smiled at me in a way that told me I was very likely going to *win* very soon, I was a haze of need and desire, one spark away from imploding.

"I don't know why we're still standing out here," she murmured, grabbing my hand and lacing our fingers together, dragging me toward the house.

Toward the porch Billie Rose had handcuffed me to.

Twice.

Because I'd needed to get my head straight and she'd somehow known that no one but Bailey was going to help me get my head out of my ass.

And it had worked.

"Shit," Bailey whispered, halting on the top step.

Tension immediately coiling in my belly. "What?" I asked, drawing her close.

"The animals. I need to get them ready for the night—"

She started to spin, started to turn for the barn, but my phone buzzed in my pocket and when I pulled it out as I followed her, glancing at the screen, my lips curved up. I drew her to a stop. "Buttercup."

"Data needs—"

I held up my cell. "Two guesses who?"

Bailey frowned.

I turned the screen so that she could read the text...

From Billie Rose.

Animals are taken care of. Now take care of my girl.

"Christ," Bailey muttered, shaking her head.

"Thus is the power of Billie Rose?"

Her mouth turned up. "Something I literally say to myself every single day."

I smoothed my free hand down her spine. "You still want to check on them anyway?"

Teeth into her bottom lip, a tinge of embarrassment in her pretty brown eyes. "Yeah," she whispered, dropping her gaze from mine.

"Buttercup."

She tugged at her hand, my fingers still laced through hers. I held fast.

"*Buttercup.*" A little firmer.

Her eyes hit mine again.

"You give Data his sugar cubes, I'll check the water buckets."

Data was her *Star Trek*-named horse who had a penchant for the little white squares. The water buckets were obvious and went along with checking the feeders and stalls. Something I never would have understood two months ago.

Something I knew now.

Something I was *happy* to know, happy to do.

Because knowing it, *doing* it, meant that I got to watch Bailey's eyes warm again, got to feel her lips brush my cheek in thanks, watch her ass, her hips sway when she strode away from me.

It meant that I was taking care of the woman I loved.

It meant...everything.

Five

He had hay in his hair and smelled like horse.

I thought that—perhaps—the combination was the best aphrodisiac on the planet.

Big, broody, sexy hockey player talking sweet to my horses, shoveling out a few stalls without complaint. Or prompting for that matter—just seeing that there was a mess that shouldn't wait until morning and cleaning it. See? An aphrodisiac.

Maybe it said something weird about me, the fact that the man got me wet just by wielding a shovel.

But...I was wet. I was horny.

I wanted to be in my bed with my man and—

Fingers along my jaw.

The smell of horse a little stronger as his body came close.

I'd been watching Data settle in for the night, mostly because I'd spent the better portion of our time in the barn staring at Axel's ass.

Hockey players had the *best* asses.

Let that be noted for the record.

Maybe it was all their time on the stationary bike or bending their knees on the ice or the squats...or just a combination of all three.

Hockey players equaled nice asses.

And Axel's was *the best*.

Probably because he was *my* hockey player and that was *my* ass and I'd readily argue with anyone about both of those facts.

Plus, is was lush and round and bitable and—

His chest pressed to my back.

Big.

All of him.

One hand dropped onto the top of the stall door next to my chest, dangerously close to my breasts, so close, in fact, that I could feel the heat from it soaking through my clothes, its proximity hardening the bud of my nipple, making the flesh tingle.

Or maybe I just had Axel detectors in my titties.

Which had me giggling.

Unfortunately, right before his mouth touched the hinge of my jaw. That was one of the spots—*the* spots—that never failed to make me shiver, to have me arching back, my softness instinctively seeking out his hard, my thighs clenching, wetness gathering, and—

"What?" he asked against my skin.

"What?" Yeah, it was a breathless question. But his body was close, his lips closer, and like one of Pavlov's dogs, the bell had been rung and I was ready.

I was *ready*.

"Why'd you giggle, buttercup?"

Oh, right.

Well, that was embarrassing. I was thinking about my boobs—referring to them as titties, no less—and Axel and Pavlov and—

I spun in his arms, rose on tiptoe, intent on his mouth—

Hands on my waist, spinning me back around, his body

coming close, pressing me into the stall door. Splinters on one side, a hard body on the other.

"Spill, honey." An order.

And, though I knew I shouldn't like it, that my body shouldn't be growing all tingly, the dampness soaking through my panties, gathering at the tops of my thighs, I liked every part of those two words. The slight growl, how his face dipped a little closer so I could feel the demand on my nape, his hands dropping onto the stall door again, caging me in completely this time.

Body close.

Axel close.

His tongue flicked out, hit skin, and a soft (and yes, breathy) moan slid from my lips. "Tell me." Another demand. Another rush of hot, damp air on the back of my neck.

And my throat unlocked, the words burst out. "My boobs are Axel Finnegan detectors. They get all tingly when you're nearby."

He froze.

I refused to be embarrassed, lifting my chin, arching my ass back so that it rubbed along the hard length of him (even though I was secretly dying inside because I'd just admitted to my titties being my tall, dark, and talented hockey player detector).

Then I was facing him again, and the heat in his bright blue eyes was a scorching summer sky, the threat of fire right there on the horizon.

One spark and everything around us would go up in flames.

My arms dropped to my sides, brushing against something soft, and I glanced down, then up, and realized that I'd missed the blanket that had been draped over the wooden wall of the stall. Right behind where my body was pressed. Not a blanket I'd put there. I wouldn't have. Data would probably eat it and then I'd be dealing with a sick horse. But it didn't surprise me that it had "magically" appeared when Axel came close, that he'd managed to position my body exactly against it.

His was a quiet kind of care (minus the *stubborn* care that came with all but forcing me to accept his help with the remodel inside).

But it was the little things like this that had eventually crumbled the walls around my heart.

That had me falling for this man and doing it deeply.

The reminder reinforced the realization I'd come to on the drive, even before he'd given me the full explanation about *Candi*.

He wasn't the kind of man who'd hurt me in that way.

He was brutally honest and had a wide self-protective streak... which usually manifested in asshole.

But once a person was allowed inside his heart there was only loyalty, only protection, only—

Love.

Then he grabbed my hand, pressed it to his granite hard erection, and I wasn't thinking about love.

Only *heat.*

"You think this thing isn't hard for you *all* the time?"

It was a rasp, his fingers flexing on mine. Not that I needed any encouragement to wrap my hand tighter around him, to feel every long, thick inch of his cock. Even without his hand tightening, I was already gripping him through his sweats, thankful that the material let me feel everything. The rock-hard length, the scalding jut, the pulsing erection. All beneath *my* hand. All for *me.*

I didn't stop with squeezing him through his pants.

I dove my hand beneath the waistband of his sweats, sliding it beneath his underwear, getting my fingers on that hard length.

I wanted my mouth on him.

I wanted to drop to my knees.

I wanted him to hit the back of my throat, to swallow the hot spurts of his cum as he fell apart.

I wanted—

His hand grasped mine, wrapping his fingers around my wrist, drawing me off him, spinning me, and dropping my palm onto the top of the railing. Then the other.

"You want it, don't you?" A velvet scrape on my nape, a dripping heat over my breasts, clinging to the hardened buds of my nipples, drizzled over my stomach, sliding between my thighs. "You want me to fuck you right here, don't you?"

Oh God, I wanted that.

So badly.

Before I could get the words out, he was on his knees. He was dragging down my pants. He was tugging my hips back.

"Christ," he muttered, palming my ass. Big, rough hands massaging. A finger dragging between my cheeks, pressing lightly against the puckered bud.

I gasped, arching back, instinctively seeking more, moaning when he gripped the top of my thong, tugged it up slightly, dragging the emerald lace through my slick folds, putting pressure both on my clit and on the sensitive flesh between my cheeks.

I needed—

A nip had me gasping again, a sting blooming on my ass before it was gently soothed by his lips and tongue.

"You want it," he murmured silkily, hand gliding over my skin, his finger tracing the line of lace. "Fuck yeah, honey, you want it."

I did.

I wanted it so badly that I was shaking.

He slid my panties down my hips, trailed his fingers back up the inside of my thighs, and then—

His tongue dipped in.

Six

I was a fucking freak.

I loved that her cheeks—both sets—had flushed when I talked about fucking her right there in the barn where anyone might come upon us. Loved that I could feel how she grew even more wet when I told her I *knew* she wanted me to fuck her right there and then.

I loved her. Period.

Not that I'd told her.

It was too soon, and after this shitshow of a day, with my tongue in her pussy, it definitely wasn't the right time.

But I'd make the time and do it soon.

And I'd make the gesture grand and worthy of her.

But, for now, I wanted to corrupt Bailey.

I wanted to fuck her with my fingers and then with my tongue and then with my cock right there with her hands clinging to the top of the stall, and then with hay prickling my back as she rode me hard, and then on that old, worn workbench that housed the saws that had brought us together...or apart and *then* together.

But first, my tongue.

I flicked it through her folds.

And even though I kept one ear on her moans, on the sexy as shit little gasps she made as she ground against my mouth and teeth and tongue, my other one was on our surroundings.

I would hear the gravel first if anyone drove or walked up the driveway.

I didn't mind playing with her, enticing her with the thought of being caught.

But she wouldn't actually want anyone to see her like this, see her vulnerable.

And I wouldn't let it happen.

And that she wasn't looking around, wasn't worried about being caught, that she was trusting me with her body open like this, lost to her pleasure...it meant more to me than perhaps anything else ever had.

I wouldn't fuck it up.

But first, I needed to fuck her.

A tug of her hips had her angled better for my mouth, and I didn't go slow or gentle or easy. It was one of my favorite activities and I dove right in, showing no mercy, sucking at her clit, tonguing her labia, slipping it inside, deep enough that my face was buried in between her cheeks, that her liquid heat was all over me—on my lips and in my beard and on my jaw and in my nose. I wanted to swim in it, to swim in her. I loved the way she smelled...everywhere. I loved when she was in my every pore. I loved when she was soaked and dripping down my chin.

But she needed to come.

Because, already, my control was fracturing.

Just weeks without her and my need was almost overwhelming.

But...Bailey first.

Always, I would put Bailey first.

Another jerk back and then I was crawling between her legs,

using my shoulders to spread them wide, spinning so that I could latch onto her clit, so that I could suck deeply.

She jolted. "*Axel.*"

Fuck, yes.

I gripped her ass, a hand on each cheek, drew her more firmly against my face, sucking hard and fast, even as more shudders wracked her frame.

Her body was talking to mine, but I didn't know that she was close because she was shaking and her pussy was convulsing around my fingers. I knew it because of how her voice broke, how my name sounded as it tumbled off her tongue over and over again. I knew it in the press of her hips, in how she ground her pussy against my face.

I knew it like I was coming myself.

And it was nearly as good.

The way her pussy grew even more slick, how tightly she clenched my fingers, her knees shaking, her head dropping back.

Her groan filling the air.

And finally, finally, her body going limp against me.

I caught her in my lap, let her rest her head against my chest, my dick still fucking aching, but not in any hurry to assuage the ache.

Because she was close. Because only I got to see her like this.

Because *I'd* made her feel good.

Because—

She moved in a rapid flash of movement that was almost too quick for me to track, and by the time I did, she was pushing me onto my back, hay prickling my skin through the fabric of my tee, her shaking fingers yanking my pants down before she clambered on top of me, slid down...

And fuck yeah, that was good.

The tight, wet clasp of her.

My cock buried deep inside.

I didn't give a fuck about the dissolution of my plans to make her come again, this time with my mouth on her tits and my fingers inside her. I didn't give a fuck that I'd been content to wait and here we were going fast again.

I didn't give a fuck—

That she was moving.

Okay, I gave *many* fucks about the last. Mostly because the way she felt was...

Everything.

"Axel," she whispered, arching back, hands hitting my thighs, lifting up and driving down. I couldn't decide where to look—watching my cock press deep into her, watching her face lit up with pleasure. And then I wasn't thinking about any of that. I wasn't even thinking about fucking her, or that it was really her fucking me, or just the fact that being inside her was better than winning a game, better than scoring that match-winning goal. I was thinking—

No.

No more thinking.

Doing.

Only doing.

I reached for the hem of her shirt and leaned up, yanking it over her head, exposing her breasts clad in dark green lace. So different from her typical function over fashion.

Not that I gave a fuck.

I could appreciate the effort, the glimpse it gave me. But I just wanted her naked. I wanted my mouth on her breasts, wanted to feel her hard nipples on my tongue.

So, I took a mental snapshot, and then I pounced.

Sucking one nipple hard, palming the other breast, bringing one hand to her ass and driving up as I yanked her down onto me. Sweat began to bead on my forehead, began to drip down my back. My abs were already on fire.

But I didn't give a fuck.

And I certainly didn't stop.

Not when my name was already rolling off her tongue and filling the air, not when she was clenching me tight inside, not when every time I pulled on her nipple, her pussy convulsed around me.

Not when I was so fucking close to coming that I knew I had to get her there and do it fast and—

I slid my hand in, gripping her ass, dipping down into the cleft between those sweet cheeks. She was soaking there, too, and my finger slid over that taut pucker, slid *into* that tighter clasp of her body.

Her rhythm faltered.

Her head shot up.

"What—"

I pressed in a little further.

Her eyes widened and I nearly stopped, nearly pulled back, but then her head dropped back, a moan tumbled out of her mouth, and her pussy went so tight around me that I saw stars.

"Axel," she groaned, that rhythm totally lost, her movements frantic and out of control and—

I was out of control too.

Feasting on her tits, thrusting my finger into her as I jerked her up and down my cock, my orgasm barreling down onto me.

No chance of slowing.

No chance of waiting.

Nothing but hitting the gas, jamming the pedal into the floor, speeding toward oblivion—

And crashing over the precipice.

"Fuck," I groaned, and then I was coming, my cock growing even harder as she milked me, as her nails dug in, as she met me thrust for thrust for thrust, our bodies seeking each other in a way that wasn't finessed or controlled but was still fucking perfect as pleasure threatened to incinerate me, to reduce me to nothing but ashes.

And I was more than happy to become dust.

SEVEN

BAILEY

Girl was going to be sore tomorrow.

That girl was me.

I was going to be sore.

Newsflash, I was a total dork.

But...I don't think I'd ever ridden a cock so hard, taken a man so deep...and that didn't even begin to take into account the finger.

Oh God, that finger.

Somehow my poor, overworked pussy convulsed, remembering the different kind of pleasure Axel's touch had wrought in me, the strange mix of pleasure and pain and needing *more*. Feeling full and also empty. Wanting another finger there. Wanting a toy there. Wanting—

His cock there.

I shivered again.

And that seemed to rouse him, his finger still inside me and flexing lightly before it gently slid free of my body. But he didn't go far, just rested his palm on my ass, his fingers between my cheeks. Did I shift slightly, body searching for him again? Yeah.

But was I *always* addicted to Axel and his body and how effectively he played mine? Definitely yes.

Was I going to fuck him again and soon? Also yes.

Just...when I felt like I had control of my limbs again.

Meanwhile, I'd collapsed against his chest, was listening to his heart pound against my ear, loving the way his arms held me so tightly.

Good enough.

This right here was good enough.

A breath that brought Axel into my nose, into my pores, into every inch of my body.

And, yeah, that was enough.

I relaxed against him.

My eyes slid closed.

———

The smell of something delicious had my stomach rumbling, and I frowned, stretching and remembering all of my soreness, a tiny groan slipping from between my lips.

A soft hand brushing back my hair.

A gentle kiss to my temple.

Who in the world had ever thought that Axel Finnegan could be gentle?

Except, he'd helped me when I tweaked my back. He'd caught me when I fell from a ladder, had gently picked glass from my body so it wouldn't cut me. He'd made sure I'd gotten home when I'd had a few too many beers (that being *two* total, which was one too many). He'd seen the state of my house and helped. Not given some bullshit "call me if you need anything." Instead, he'd stepped up, had done *something*.

So yeah, even though the man could crush someone on the ice, could be an asshole in real life, I knew he could be gentle.

Because he was gentle with *me*.

"Barn fucking a bad idea?" he asked, tucking a strand of hair behind my ear.

My mouth tipped up, eyes peeling open and taking in my sexy hockey player. His hair was a mess, and his shirt had been full of hay, so he'd taken it off—then hadn't bothered to put a new one on (oh the humanity and my eyes, my poor eyes)—and I...wanted to jump his bones, wanted to collapse in bed together and talk about nothing and everything.

I wanted him.

With me.

Always.

But he'd be leaving in the morning.

Sigh.

"I don't think us fucking is *ever* a bad idea," I said, forcing my tone to be light.

Hot blue eyes. A wicked grin. "Now, that might be the smartest thing you've ever said."

I growled, managed to rouse my limp limbs, and poked him lightly in the chest. "Jerk."

"Sexy, smart." A kiss to the tip of my nose. "*Mine.*"

"Hmph." But I didn't argue, and maybe considering that my ex who'd claimed me as his had been in my driveway just a couple of hours before, warning me of all the risks that came from men and their penchant for claiming, I should have rebuffed the statement.

But...

Axel wasn't Colt.

And as much as I should be leery of men and relationships...I'd carried Colt's shit for too long. And, frankly, I'd been to too many therapy sessions, had worked too hard to get my life and mind and heart together after Colt to go backward now.

There was a time I couldn't even think his name, couldn't imagine letting the good man in this room into my life.

I wasn't going back there.

Wasn't going back to isolating myself and living in the shadows.

Life was good, and I was going to embrace it.

'Cause, God knew, shit was about to get fucked if my parents had shown up on my doorstep.

Right.

Didn't want to think about them or Colt. Not when Axel was here and had to leave in the morning and I didn't know when I'd see him next.

"How'd I get to bed?" I asked as Axel bent away from me and set the plates he had balanced on his free arm on the nightstand. I remembered enjoying my personal Axel pillow, but that was it.

"You were out," he said by way of explanation, turning back and sliding in so that our bodies faced each other, our hips touching, his big, broad palm resting between my legs and reminding me all over again that I didn't want food.

I wanted him.

But I wanted *all* of him.

So while I didn't close my legs—that would both reveal too much *and* trap his hand against me (thus undoing any of my progress in wanting to know more of his big, juicy brain instead of his big...juicy—*ew*—hard—*yeah, that was better*—cock)—and while I was hyperaware (*hyper!*) of its proximity to all the parts of me he was very good at rousing to liquid attention, I forced myself to focus on him, on us, on our conversation.

I lifted my brows. "And me being out means what?"

"It means you're little and I'm strong." His smile was cocky now. "So, I carried you in."

"You do know that I have two feet, right?" I nodded toward the body parts in question. "And those feet are attached to legs that could have walked myself into the house."

"You were *out*." Axel didn't seem bothered by my tart tone. In fact, he seemed to be fighting a smile. "And since you weren't using those feet or those legs, I used my *two*"—the emphasis on *two* would have driven me crazy a few months ago, it was so condescending, but since I knew him, and since I was dishing out the sass just as heartily, his tone had me biting back a smile instead—"arms to carry you up into bed and set about rousing you by showing off my culinary delights."

I cocked my head to the side. "Set about?"

A shrug, though his cheeks took on the barest hint of pink.

"Culinary delights?"

Another shrug, more pink. "I might be dating a woman who is a Trekkie, but I also know she likes certain books."

Delight—of the non-culinary variety—bubbled up inside me. "And?"

"And maybe those books are..."

I grinned, clapped my hands together. "Amazing? Hot? Make you want to get me in a big, puffy dress so that you can take advantage of me in a carriage or pin me to an alley wall, flip up my skirts, and—"

"Right," he growled.

I blinked.

But didn't get the chance to actually get any words out, not when he was moving.

One jerk had the blankets yanked down, revealing my naked body.

The next movement had him on top of me, his lips stopping just a hairsbreadth away from mine.

"What about your culinary delights?" I asked, and was it breathless?

Yes.

I had Axel Finnegan pinning me to the bed, his blue eyes full of storm clouds and lightning, and I was very much looking forward to being caught up in the maelstrom, so *of course* my question was breathless.

He snagged my wrist in another of those quick movements, bringing it to his mouth, tongue flicking out and tasting the tiny tattoo I had there. "I want to know what this means," he said in his velvet rasp.

"I—"

Before my answer could fully form, he lifted my arm higher, over my head, wrapping my fingers around the cool metal bar that ran along the bottom of my headboard.

"But later."

He lifted my other arm, encouraged those fingers to wrap around the bar, too.

"Wh—?"

"First"—he snagged something from the plate on the night-stand—"my culinary delights."

My lungs were struggling from the onslaught of his body, from the ache in my breasts, fully on display with my hands gripping that metal bar, my nipples all but begging for his mouth, but when I caught sight of what was in the little bowl he dipped his fingers into, I glanced into those thundercloud eyes, into the flurry of lightning sparking through his irises. I was holding a metal bar in the middle of a giant storm, all but calling for the cloud's electricity to coalesce onto me...

And I smiled.

Bring on the storm.

EIGHT

"I hate that you have to go," she whispered, arms tight around my waist, face buried in my chest.

Right against my heart.

That beat for her.

Only for her.

Something that never should have happened, considering all the walls I built, reinforced with concrete, with barbed wire, encircled with a giant ass moat that was filled with toxic waste-laced water and crocodiles that had mutated into freakish beasts.

Maybe I was watching too much *Star Trek* and it was mixing oddly with those historical romance novels I'd become secretly addicted to.

Women.

They seriously fucked a man up.

Except, even as I was thinking it, my heart smiled.

Yup. I wasn't even going to kick my own ass for thinking that bit of trite nonsense. It was the fucking truth.

This woman.

This woman fucked me up in the best possible way.

But I still had to go.

I had practice that afternoon and a long drive to make before that.

"I know, buttercup."

Her head tilted back, soft brown eyes hitting mine. "We didn't get to talk much."

No. We hadn't. Between the barn and then her nap and my *culinary delights,* we hadn't had energy for much talking when we'd finally collapsed.

After a shower.

After changing the sticky sheets.

Because my *culinary delights* mostly extended to breakfast.

A nip to the hinge of her jaw. "Keep the syrup warm for me."

Her lips tipped up. "I think I have a Costco trip in my future to make sure we don't run out."

I kissed them. "The vat I ordered is coming on two-day shipping."

Now she grinned. And that was better. I didn't like leaving her, but I liked leaving her even less when she was sad, and even *more* less with her parents and asshole ex potentially in town and ready to unleash trouble.

I knew Billie Rose would rally the town to keep an eye out.

But I knew that I was going to take further precautions.

I had to.

I couldn't be fucking states or a country away and not know she was safe. I couldn't do my job with worry sitting heavy on my shoulders.

I already hated that she wasn't in San Francisco, waiting for me to get back from a road trip or watching in the team box with the other WAGs.

"You'll be careful?" I asked.

Her palm came to my cheek, and I felt the gentle touch like it was a brand on my skin. "I'll be careful," she promised.

Turning my head, I kissed the inside of her wrist, kissed the tattoo there. "We talked enough for me to know what *this* means."

Now her cheeks flushed.

Because I'd learned something about her.

Learned that the apple on her wrist wasn't an homage to Data's second favorite treat, but it was an homage to her dream.

She wanted to teach high school English.

I couldn't imagine why.

Teenagers were assholes and getting them to read serious books rather than consuming thirty-second TikTok videos seemed to be a lesson in futility. But then again, she'd gotten a dumbass hockey player to watch *Star Trek* and read historical romance novels, so Bailey could probably get those high schoolers to do anything.

"It's silly," she'd whispered. "I mean, I didn't even get my credentials and now I have the ranch—"

"It's not," I'd whispered back. "It's not silly to dream."

And when she'd looked into my eyes, I knew that she saw.

Knew that she saw how much she'd impacted *my* dream. Knew that she understood I was demanding that she not give up on hers.

And for once, she didn't give me shit about demanding.

She'd just laid her head back down on my chest, wrapped her arm around my middle, and my heart had smiled again.

"Don't give up, okay?" I whispered now, pressing another kiss to the mark.

"I still have at least a year before the ranch will be out of the financial hell-hole my parents left it in, and that's not including anything that might happen with them showing up." She dropped her head to my chest. "I'm trying not to worry about how fucked up this is going to get—"

Fingers on her jaw, tilting her head back so that she would look at me. "Buttercup."

"Horses and cows are easier than people," she muttered.

"You won't hear me arguing with you about that."

Her nose wrinkled. "At least you get to shoot pucks at them."

Fuck, she was cute.

I bent and kissed those little lines creasing her adorable upturned nose. "True." A kiss to her forehead. "Next time I'm in River's Bend, I'll pull some strings and get you a couple of hockey players to practice shooting pucks at."

She laughed.

I had to taste it, taste her smile.

So I did, and it filled a part of me that I hadn't even known was empty, not until Bailey had come into my life.

When we'd broke apart, chests heaving, her hand found my jaw again. "I love that you make me laugh."

I love...

Those two words slid through me, weighty and intense and fucking perfect.

Minus the fact that they hadn't ended with *you*.

But after the shitshow of yesterday, I'd take making her laugh any day of the week, any *moment* of the fucking day.

"I love—"

Her breath caught, and I pressed her hand to my face, imprinting her touch on my skin, so I could carry it with me while we were apart.

"I love," I said again, "that I can do that for you."

A glimmer of disappointment in her chocolate brown eyes before it was dutifully tucked away.

Because it was too soon.

Because we had too much going on.

She deserved better. More. *Everything.*

I smothered my impatience.

Slow. So I didn't fuck this up.

Because I wanted to keep her forever.

"We're going to be okay," I said.

Because I *wouldn't* fuck this up.

The disappointment was gone, and then she was pasting on a smile I knew was as much for her benefit as it was for mine. "I know."

Determination and a spine of steel.

Part of why I loved her. But only part because there wasn't anything I didn't love about her—not her stubborn pride, not the way she was terrible at accepting help and exceptional at giving it, not the way she cared for her animals and the people in her life who'd made it past that treacherous stubborn pride.

I could go on.

But I was just prolonging the pain.

I had to leave.

She knew it, too. "Go," she whispered, and kissed me. "I'm going to ride Data. Something," she added, dropping back onto her heels, face gentle and warm, and I knew *that* was what I was going to be dreaming of tonight, the way she was looking at me in that moment. "I get to do because my hot, hockey-playing boyfriend got up early and mucked stalls for me."

"Buttercup—"

She reached behind me, tugged open the driver's side door. "Go, honey."

I inhaled, fought down my protest, and got in the car.

Not before I stole another kiss, though. One hot and *warm* (yes, there was a difference between hot and warm—one was for my dick, the other for my heart) and long enough to tide us both over.

"See you soon," she whispered, her fingers clinging to mine.

I nodded, forcing myself to peel my hand away. "Text me when you're back from your ride with Data."

She inclined her head.

And then I didn't have any other reason to delay, or couldn't think of any, anyway.

So, I pulled the Band-Aid, making it easier on both of us,

closing my door, starting the engine, reversing slowly out of the driveway so as not to disrupt the gravel.

And then I drove away from the woman I loved.

And I hated every fucking minute of it.

———

When I hit the highway and cell coverage wasn't spotty, I called Joel.

My former teammate was a real ballbuster and general pain in the ass.

But he was big and scary and could handle himself.

He was also a dog who'd made it most of his life's duty to score as much pussy as possible. Pucks and pussy. That had been our motto.

Before Bailey had pulled a shotgun on me.

Before Billie Rose had helped me sort my shit with a pair (two?) of handcuffs.

Before I'd realized that so much of what was stopping me from achieving what I wanted was in my own fucking head.

Joel was still living that motto, albeit without tearing up the town.

Which I approved of.

Once I'd allowed myself, I'd found that River's Bend was pretty dope.

Or maybe it was the woman living on the outskirts of it.

Or—

"Hello?" Joel's voice was groggy.

No doubt because the guys had played last night and then celebrated their win (or loss) with booze and chicks.

"Hey, it's me."

"Axel?" A grunt, fumbling in the background. "Christ, do you know what time it is?"

"Yeah. I'm sorry to..." A feminine protest in the background that had me biting back laughter. Fuck. Some things didn't change. "*Interrupt*, but I need a favor."

A beat of quiet.

But then there was the sound of material sliding against material, of footsteps on hardwood floor, of a door closing.

"What's up, man?" Joel rasped.

"It's about Bailey..." And then I spent the next couple of minutes explaining about her ex and what I knew—which wasn't nearly everything, not all that had he'd done to Bailey, but even just explaining the bare bones that I *did* know along with what had happened the day before had my blood boiling all over again.

Joel cursed several times during my explanation.

I knew he would.

As much pussy as he chased, as much as he liked to let it rip and tie one on, he had three sisters and if any of their husbands had treated them like Colt had treated Bailey...

They'd be six feet under.

"I'm not there," I finished. "I mean even when the team is playing at home, I'm still not nearly close enough. I know Billie Rose and the rest of the town will look after her, but..."

"You're not there," he finished for me.

"Yeah," I whispered.

A breath, but then Joel's voice was fierce. "I'll—*we'll* be there when we can. Keep an eye out. Make sure that fucking harpy of a mayor doesn't slack in her duty of keeping an eye out, too."

Even though the last made me smile because I knew from first-hand experience how much of a handful Billie Rose could be (though I'd say less harpy and more of a confident, definitely scary Cupid), I didn't laugh.

Because this might have been the most serious conversation Joel and I had ever had.

And that made me sad.

How much I'd been holding back from my teammates.

How much I'd missed out on because I'd been so good at isolating myself.

I wouldn't make that same mistake with my new teammates—Brit and the rest of the Gold crew wouldn't let that happen even if I tried—but I wouldn't have the chance to go back and have a do-over with these guys.

I'd just corrupted them and led them astray and then went onto the Big Show.

Not entirely fair to me, I knew.

They were adults and made their own choices, and once I'd gotten my shit together, I'd encouraged them to do the same.

But it wasn't enough.

"Thanks, man," I said, and I knew my tone revealed too fucking much.

But, for once, Joel didn't dive into the weakness and give me shit. Instead, he just grunted back and said, "No thanks needed. Now I'm awake at a godawful hour and have a hot, naked chick in my bed. I'm going back to do what I'm best at."

I snorted. "Giving orgasms?"

"No." A beat. "Playing fucking Twister."

I blinked.

"Get it?" A chuckle. "Playing *Fucking* Twister."

Ah. There was the Joel I knew. Lame jokes, dirty mind, and all booming laughter through my car's speakers.

"God, I hope she wins," I muttered.

"Oh, she will," he countered.

Before I could quip back, he disconnected.

Probably for the best.

"*Fucking* Twister."

Laughing, I shook my head.

Mostly because I was jealous.

And maybe because a new activity for Bailey and me had just been scratched onto my mental To Do List.

To *Do*.

I grinned.

Fuck, one conversation with Joel and I was turning into a child.

But I still drove with a smile on my face for the rest of the way back to San Francisco.

To. *Do*.

Heh.

Nine

BAILEY

The rolling hills were one of my favorite parts.

But most especially this time of year.

It was cool, mist clinging to the grass, glimmering from the sun rising in the east, turning them into tiny crystal-like statues. Like something my grandmother would have collected if they really *were* crystal and sparkly and something she could have picked up from River's Marketplace, the same store downtown that carried everything from sweatshirts to tubes that could be inflated and rode down the river to tiny crystal statues.

Statues that definitely would be collecting dust on my shelves.

I much preferred to admire them like this.

With the breeze in my hair and through those long blades of grass, sending both waving.

I could control only one of those—the former—and spent a minute tying it back, letting Data have her head, have a bit of freedom.

Not that I was ever tight on the reins.

Not with Data.

We'd been riding together for long enough that we didn't need that communication.

We were one.

And I needed the bit of freedom myself, to not have to be in charge, to be able to pause and enjoy the quiet...and reflect.

The last twenty-four hours had been...

Insanity.

A fucking roller coaster.

Christ.

My parents. *Colt.*

Colt, I had no fucking clue what he wanted. He hadn't contested the divorce, hadn't sought me out after that night in the rain, when he'd left me with broken ribs and a swollen jaw and split lip and black eyes and a mild concussion.

He'd just...pushed me to my breaking point then had discarded me like trash.

So, him being there, him being with my *parents,* was a fucking mystery.

My parents' motivations, on the other hand, were obvious.

They were out of money. Again.

The ranch was doing well, and it was—cue jazz hands—freshly renovated. Of course, my mom would want to spend time in a house that had a suite she'd designed, and the remainder of the house was almost on par with that luxury she desired.

No more floral on floral on floral couch.

No more old shag carpeting that grabbed every crumb.

Sleek wood floors. New tile in the bathrooms. New cabinets *and* appliances in the kitchen. New furniture. New carpet. New electrical and plumbing. Paid for by Axel. All selected by me and Dessie and Margaret, who was River's Bend's only interior designer.

Gramps's house was no longer the explosion of the eighties and before.

It was *mine* now.

And my mom wanted her talons in it.

I needed to talk to my lawyer, find out if my parents had any right to the house. I'd gotten a loan, bought their portion of the property outright. Billie Rose didn't even have a share of the property itself. She got a small cut of the profits, but that was the extent of my aunt's legal ties to Russet Ranch.

But my parents shouldn't have any say, any claim. They shouldn't be *here*.

Someone might think that my dad would give a fuck about the ranch.

It was technically his legacy, after all—though Gramps had only left him a third (something I'd found out when I'd begun desperate proceeding to buy their share so Russet Ranch didn't go under and was sold to developers).

But I'd never been able to figure out *what* my father actually cared about. He just...existed on the outskirts of my life, living his own, and so unattached that he made my mother look like Mom of the Year.

He certainly didn't give a fuck about the legacy—he'd hated bringing me up to the ranch during the summers, had left that to my mother or made Gran or Gramps of Billie's parents pick me up. He didn't give a fuck about his parents—I'd never seen him visit, not once. He didn't give a shit about me—he'd never been bothered to check a homework assignment, to go to a school activity. Hell, he hadn't been bothered to get me to school at *all*.

I suppose I should be happy that at least my mother pretended sometimes.

She'd driven me to school when I was too little to walk myself.

She'd cooked me dinner before I figured out how to pour myself a bowl of cereal and not dump it all over the floor, and...I'm sure there had to have been a few other things, even if they didn't spring immediately to mind.

The point was, I'd survived to adulthood.

And while I'd done it mostly eating cereal, or consuming the remnants of my friends' lunches at school, and learning how to wash my own clothes in kindergarten...

I was here.

And I'd had Gran and Gramps.

I had Data and Billie Rose and maybe I'd had to sell my pet cow, Picard, to a petting zoo so I could afford the premium streaming package to watch my boyfriend play hockey.

But I had a boyfriend who played hockey.

And he was nice and sexy and had a big cock.

And he got up early with me so that all my big chores were done and I could take Data out.

And maybe he was a fucking miracle.

Or maybe he was just *Axel*.

I smiled, sitting in this quiet moment with the waving grass and sun peeking up over the hills.

Pausing so that I could soak it in, hold it close, lock it up safe.

Because I had the feeling that this peace that Axel had given me, the small slice of happy and contentment that he'd managed to carve out for me wasn't going to continue for long.

———

"And I'll have the Caesar salad with dressing on the side and extra—"

"Cracked black pepper, Parmesan, and none of the stemmy leaves," Bonnie finished, gaze flicking up to mine, her pale brown eyes twinkling as she took our lunch order. A secondary perk of the hot boyfriend with the big dick who got up early and helped with chores was that I had enough time to actually socialize every once in a while. Which, I supposed, could be good or bad. But today it was good. I loved Billie and was happy to take her to lunch for all her help with my house. "I've known you for almost thirty years, Rosie girl. I've got your salad order memorized. *And* your ice water with lemons and not *too much* ice covered," she added, writing a note on her pad.

"I just like what I like," Billie murmured, and strangely, she looked a little insecure.

Which was an odd look on my typically assured aunt's face.

"Of course you do," Bonnie said, patting Billie's hand, whose expression quickly cleared and returned to its normal commanding presence, making me almost think that I'd imagined it.

I *must* have imagined it.

Because then she said, in normal Billie Rose fashion, "I know you've got it covered, but I'm still going to ask for rolls hot from the oven and extra butter."

Bonnie laughed, tucked her pen behind her ear. "Of course you are, honey bun."

A wink at me. "The special for you, booboo?"

I nodded, passed over my menu. "Sounds good. Thanks, Bonnie."

"Anytime, girls."

She turned away, moved over to the large window so she could call their order to Deke, who was on that day, and I was watching her, laughing at the sass she tossed the chef (who also happened to be her husband), when Billie Rose asked, "What's the special?"

I turned back, shrugged. "I don't know."

Billie gaped at me.

Literally gaped.

But she recovered quickly, as was her power. "You *don't* know."

I sat back, smothered a laugh. "Nope."

"But—but—" Her lips pressed together, fell open again. "But how can you just order and no *know?* What if you don't like it— What if—"

I let her sputter for a few more moments and then took pity on her, covering her hand with my own, squeezing it lightly. "Deke doesn't make anything I don't like to eat." A shrug. "Plus, there isn't much that I don't like to eat, anyway, and everything the Deke makes..."

"You like," Billie finished, as though she were giving the answer to the most baffling question in the universe.

Now I chuckled. "Yup."

"I—"

Bonnie saved me from further explanation and Billie from having her head explode because of it by bringing our drinks— water with lemons and not too much ice for my aunt and a Diet Coke for me.

See?

She knew her shit and would take care of me.

I smiled sweetly at Billie Rose before sipping from my glass.

And then I took pity on her.

"Tell me where we're at with the Winter Festival."

A pained look. Because she wanted to gab about her plans. I knew she did, knew how much she loved putting on the festivals. But she was worried about me and trying to be a good friend and aunt. "We should talk about your parents and Colt." A beat. "And Axel."

We *should*.

But I didn't want to (and yeah, I said that in my head like a whining toddler).

"Later," I promised. "Right now, I want to hear if the City Council approved the ice rink."

Billie's eyes flared with excitement.

And then the excitement went verbal.

I heard about the ice rink (approved of course) and the carriage rides and the brand-spanking-new lights and decoration contest (using donated potted pines that would be planted when spring-time came around, making the whole contest competitive and eco-friendly, and Billie Rose to an absolute T).

I heard about hot cocoa stabds (and permission to sell a spiked variety for those twenty-one and older).

I heard how she commandeered more Rush skaters to volunteer their time as ice attendants.

I heard about all the small details that made Billie Rose the perfect mayor for River's Bend—the care, the love, the enthusiasm, they all swept me along.

Until I was volunteering for more than I should.

Until I was going to be all-in on the festival, rather than voluntold.

Until I knew that so much had changed inside me because I never *ever* would have been able to open myself up to her, to the town, to the event—too many painful memories, too much of a reminder of what I'd missed.

And I knew that change had begun with Axel.

No. With Billie Rose.

Because she'd handcuffed Axel to my porch.

Ah.

The sweet, *sweet* stories of love and inner growth...and shotguns and handcuffs and crocodile death-rolling my way into a relationship that I would one day tell the grandkids.

But I was thinking about grandkids...

And not running screaming, like my hair was on fire, from the diner.

See? Progress.

I was making it.

I was making a *lot* of it.

So maybe my intuition on the hill was wrong, maybe this would perfect and happily-ever-after.

Maybe the peace would hold.

And if it didn't maybe I'd be able to easily navigate my way through it, considering all that inner growth.

Maybe.

I smiled, ate my food when Bonnie brought it.

And for the record, Deke's Reuben was incredible.

TEN

"Yeah, yeah, yeah, *yeah!*" Coop yelled for the puck, but I'd already seen him breaking for the net, watched him slide in and lift his stick in preparation for the one-timer.

My stick was already moving, almost before my mind was.

The puck sailed toward Coop, hovering a few inches above the ice before dropping down right where I'd wanted it—

A couple of feet in front of him, so my teammate could pick it up and keep moving without breaking stride or losing speed.

Ben, one of the newer guys on the roster, whistled.

Oddly, he was sporting a black eye, and though I didn't ask, I knew it had something to do with the fact that he'd been caught in Josh's sister's bed.

Normally, I would have thought that would implode the locker room.

And, not gonna lie, there was plenty of tension there, but no one was putting fists through walls, no one was excluding Ben, no one was cornering anyone in the showers or the hall or an empty corner of the training suite and beating him to shit.

Oh, Josh's face still turned murderous every time he looked at his teammate...

But Ben was doing a good job of laying low, and the guys—*all* of them, including Josh—were letting him.

No cheap shots on the ice.

No blacklisting from group hangouts.

Just dirty looks and the occasional blip of tension in the locker room.

Yeah, these guys were too fucking healthy.

And I loved it.

I hadn't been this happy, work-wise, ever. I hadn't been this happy *hockey*-wise probably from the moment I stopped playing just for fun and started playing competitively.

It was...the dream.

The *dream*.

"Hell of a pass," Ben muttered, thwacking me in the shins with his stick.

A mere love tap, that was all.

Grinning, I tapped him back as we watched Coop finish the rest of the drill, the two "opponents" working on their coverage as he danced with the puck in the corner.

Fucker had a featherlight touch with the biscuit, and he was fast as hell.

And he just kept getting better with age.

I was jealous as fuck, but I was also taking note of every single pointer I could.

Coop had years on me—both in age and in the league—but he'd overcome injury and mental blocks and was one of the best players in the league.

So, I'd be stupid to *not* soak up every single thing I could.

"He's got good hands," I muttered and, look at me go, being all modest and shit.

Grinning, seeing right through me, Ben tapped my shins again and skated off, lining up to take his turn.

"Give me another of those pretty passes, Balls!" Ben yelled.

A man helps out with *one* Harvest Festival, tells a couple of pretend fortunes using a fake crystal ball...and is saddled with the nickname *Balls* for the rest of his life.

The man was me.

My nickname was Balls.

Sigh.

But I'd take the ribbing.

Because it meant that I was one of them.

I snagged a couple of pucks, lined up to be ready for Ben when he started the drill. On the whistle, he took off, and I waited... waited...waited then—

Pass.

Right then.

It was the right *time*.

Ben slid through the first defenseman, snagged the puck on the bounce and—

I winced when Josh squeezed Ben out on the boards, their bodies and the subsequent collision making the glass rattle.

It wasn't a game-grade hit.

But it was a reminder that Josh still wasn't all that happy with the fact that he'd found Ben naked in bed with his sister.

Ben just took the hit—luckily rolling with it and not escalating. Probably because he had a younger sister himself and knew what it was like to be protective. Also, probably, because Josh might be pissed, be a big brother in every cell of his body, but he was a good captain, and he wouldn't jeopardize the team.

Not when his sister made it clear she was an adult who made her own decisions.

One of which was that sleeping with Ben had been consensual and—

"Whatcha thinking about, rook?" Brit asked, coming up behind me.

I turned to the goalie, her helmet propped back on her head, her wide smile on full display. "That Ben is lucky Josh isn't a loose cannon."

She grinned, that smile growing somehow wider. "Definitely lucky."

"Though the black eye..."

"Probably the least of his concerns," she said, "considering how they were discovered. Joshie can throw a mean ass right hook. I've seen it from the crease more than a few times." A laugh. "Just another reason that I'm glad goalies aren't out here fighting." She buffed her nails on her shoulder.

"Just saying, goalies *do* fight."

She let her hand fall to her side, shoving it into her glove before nodding sharply so that her helmet dropped into place. A practiced motion that spoke of years of playing. "Just saying"—she rolled her shoulders—"*this* goalie doesn't fight."

"Just watches the Neanderthals duke it out and then sneakily cup checks any asshole who skates through your crease."

A flash of straight, white teeth. "It's *my* crease."

I laughed.

She gave my shin guards a tap. "Keep it up, Balls. You're doing good."

"Thanks, Brit," I murmured.

The whistle trilled again, and she moved in to take her turn on the drill, swapping spots with our backup goalie, Harrison.

Coach Calle kept me on the passing station, and I dished pucks out to Rome, Lucas, Will, and Kaydon before Coop swapped out with me. I did my time grinding it out on the boards, managed to do a couple of good moves and get a decent shot on net—

Which Brit cursed me out for, since she really had to scrabble to save it.

Though she did the cursing with a smile, and I was grinning as the f-bombs rained down. Because it was good, it meant *I* was doing good.

Something I wouldn't have been able to do if not for Bailey, if not for Brit, if not for Billie Rose.

B-named angels.

Which was a thought I knew I was *never* going to let out of my head.

If any of those three caught wind of it, the shit-giving was going to be unbearable.

But it was the truth.

And fuck, I missed *my* B-named angel. I missed *my* Bailey.

A half day away from her and I was a mopey asshole.

Probably why I missed the puck flying at my head. "Look alive, Balls!"

I didn't look alive. I was thinking about the intervening B-named women in my life, and was knee-deep (mind-deep?) in my ever-growing list of sexual fantasies I wanted to act out with the woman I loved—was fucking her on skates doable? How about on her horse?

I was thinking about *all* of that.

So, I didn't see Brit launch the puck.

Didn't see it lofting through the air toward me.

Didn't see it until it was nearly at my head, and by then it was too late to dodge.

It beaned me right in the visor—and let me thank the hockey gods for whoever had decided they were now mandatory on every player's helmet. But I didn't thank them for anything else, not when I jerked in surprise, leaned too far back on my skates and promptly went ass over tea kettle.

My ass hurt like hell.

My mind spun with the sudden turn of events.

Then Brit was in front of me, concern on her face...except it was concern mixed with amusement. So much amusement that she was having a hard time holding back her laughter.

"I—"

"Oh, shit," Brit said, bending over and resting her hands on her knees. "Fuck, I didn't think you would fall like that and—" A giggle escaped. "I mean, you went *down.*"

Kayden swatted her, but he was biting back a smile.

As were Coop and Rome.

"My ass," I moaned, rolling to my side. "Good God, *my ass.*"

Brit's head jerked up, her eyes going wide. "Oh shit, are you hurt? Like really hurt?"

"My pride? My ego? My *ass?*" I quipped.

She choked.

"Yeah, maybe," I finished.

And...she lost any hold on her laughter, busting up until she was collapsing beside me on the ice, her body shaking with it, her smile and amusement infectious.

And I couldn't hold out.

I lost it, too.

"Maybe we shouldn't call you *Balls,*" Logan said, extending a hand once Brit and I had gotten ourselves under control again.

I grabbed it, hauled myself up, ignoring my aching ass (and it *fucking* hurt since there was barely any padding in that area... mostly because professional hockey players didn't usually land square on their asses...because they could do things like, well, *skate*).

"Maybe his name should be B&A," Coop called once I'd gotten vertical, Brit beside me, ice clinging to the ends of her ponytail.

I glanced over.

Coop's eyes were dancing.

And, honestly, the rest of the guys were either laughing, amused, or smiling.

Christ. I braced as I turned back to Brit, mouthed, "B&A?"

She lifted her brows, shook her head in answer.

Coop clarified for me. "Balls and Ass."

My groan bubbled up in my throat, and out of the corner of my eye, I saw Brit start shaking with mirth.

The guys busted up, their laughter ringing across the ice, filling in spots inside me that I hadn't even begun to know were empty.

And, fuck it all, I started laughing, too.

ELEVEN

BAILEY

The Gold were playing, and I was watching it on my new TV, sitting on my new couch, next to my aunt and Dessie.

My bare toes were buried in the plush carpet.

(Beneath which was the extra thick pad that Margaret had insisted upon...and I wasn't hating, especially since it felt like I was walking on clouds anytime I made my way across this room).

"I think I'm actually getting the hang of this whole hockey thing," I said, finally able to follow the puck on the screen without having to search for it.

"Yeah?" Billie Rose murmured. "Wanna tell me what that whistle was for?"

The ref had called the play on the ice to a stop...and I had no clue why.

"Um..." I began, trying to discern the gestures and not making heads or tails of them.

"High-sticking," Dessie said, eyes glued to the screen. "Four minutes because your hot hockey player is bleeding."

"*What?*" I gasped, jerking up and watching the camera pan to Axel.

There was a woman in a black polo, Gold logo embroidered above the breast pocket, holding a piece of gauze to his nose.

And yup, that was blood.

A lot of it.

"Is it normal for a nose to bleed that much?" I asked, heart pounding so hard it felt like it was in my throat.

"If it gets smacked with a stick," Dessie said dryly, "then I would think so. I think it caught his lip too." A beat. "Though, for the record, since we're watching it happen on live TV, I think we can say it can bleed that much. It's not like they're CGIing things out there."

I threw a pillow at her. "Asshole."

"You love me." She grinned, threw it back. "Also, look at my friend," she said all too innocently, all too sweetly. "She's all concerned for her pretty, hockey boyfriend's face."

"Dessie," I warned, glaring at her before turning back to the screen and watching Axel mop up his nose and mouth.

The trainer said something, gestured to the hall, and the camera cut away.

Probably because they'd reached the max of how much blood could be shown on national television.

But I wanted the camera to pan back.

I wanted to see him, make sure he was okay.

And, Christ, it was just a bloody nose. Why was I so worried?

Because I was here and he was there and I was hopelessly, pathetically in love with that man.

Ugh.

I was turning into one of those sappy, lovestruck women.

"I need another beer," I muttered, pushing to my feet and heading for the kitchen.

"Me, too," Dessie said.

"More wine for me," Billie Rose said, lifting her glass.

"What, am I your waiter?" I snapped.

"Chilled, please, honey," Billie Rose replied, not cowed by my tone in the least. Hell, the order didn't even leave her voice.

Sighing, I plucked the wine glass from her hand and took it into the kitchen, grabbing the bottle of white from a local winery that Billie had stashed in the fridge. Then two beers. Then a plastic container of salsa. A bag of chips and a container of caramel corn from the pantry (now fully stocked since Axel had groceries delivered to me every Sunday afternoon).

I was balancing everything and moving back into the family room, all while trying to pretend that my gaze didn't keep going to the TV, searching for Axel.

Still, hopelessly, pathetically in love with that man.

Ugh.

Not that I'd expected my feelings to change in the five minutes I was away from the space, not that I wanted them to.

I just...was falling in deeper and deeper and deeper and—

That was scary.

I was scared.

And—the pieces in my mind clicked into place—that was okay.

Big feelings. Big changes. Big—

I glanced back to the screen, saw that Axel was back on the bench, dried blood caked around his nostrils, a bruise already forming on either side of his nose, a cut on his lip. His eyes met the camera, and it seemed like he was staring right at me, then I knew he was *looking* at me when he mouthed, "I'm good, buttercup."

I sucked in a breath, turned away from the TV, eyes stinging.

My gaze caught on Billie Rose's, and I didn't miss the approval in my aunt's eyes. Nor did I miss the pride that took up nearly as much space.

She'd started this, after all.

No surprise that she'd be proud of herself.

She should be, I supposed.

She played me and Axel both like puppets, guiding us right to each other, putting her matchmaking skills to work, and then stepping back at the right time so that Axel and I could sort out our own shit.

"Billie," I began.

But there was a knock at the door.

Frowning, I turned toward the hall, not able to see much since the curtain was drawn. Though the lights were on, illuminating the porch—I wasn't going to be too careful with Colt around—I couldn't see anything more than a few shadows through that swathe of fabric.

My gut clenched.

But then I relaxed.

If it was my parents, my mother, her shrill voice would be coming through the glass.

And if it was Colt...

My intestines tangled again, fear having turned into thorns that were stabbing my veins. I shoved it all down, took a breath.

If it was Colt, my shotgun was nearby.

"I'll get it," Billie Rose murmured, taking the popcorn and chips from me, setting them all on the table.

"No," I whispered, setting the two beers down and handing Billie her glass, plunking the salsa next to the chips. "I've got it."

Heart in my throat.

Pulse beating painfully in my veins.

Fingers grazing the shotgun mounted on the wall right near the door as my other hand reached for the handle, turning it and...

Not Colt.

Not my parents.

A big, broad hockey player.

One of the shadows shifted.

No. Make that *two* big, broad hockey players.

Neither of which being the one I actually wanted to have

somehow teleported himself from his game to be standing on these wooden planks.

Shaking myself, I managed only, "Umm..."

I thought I'd reached my limit of big, broad hockey players showing up on my porch.

But apparently there were two more in my future.

"Hey, babycakes," the bigger one with blond hair and green eyes said. If I was remembering right, his name was Joel and he'd been Axel's second in command, though lately he'd seemed to have laid off...well, the *laying* of every single female in town.

Another man was next to him, also clearly a hockey player based on his build and the Rush-branded hoodie he was wearing, though his name didn't come readily to mind.

I'd never really watched hockey before getting with Axel, and that meant if the players weren't gossiped about around town, then I didn't really know them.

It was the big one and the bigger one and...*this* one.

Joel clapped me on the shoulder. "I'm sure you're disappointed that we're not naked—"

A sniff from behind me.

I glanced back and saw Billie Rose had come into the hallway and was standing behind me (of course she had). Dessie was just a few paces behind her, leaning against the wall, ankles crossed, curiosity on her face...as opposed to the fury on Billie's.

"You shouldn't be here," she snapped, moving so that she was next to me.

"The big man asked me to keep an eye out for her so that's what we're here to do."

I felt my eyes go wide. "What?"

The other man stepped forward slightly, extended his hand toward me. "Hi, Bailey. I'm Ryan. I don't think we've officially met."

I shook my head. "No, I don't think so either," I said softly. Ryan hadn't hung out with the other Rush guys, not that I'd seen anyway. Not...that I'd been in town, hanging in the bars to say that with one hundred percent confidence.

"Axel asked if we could check in on you every once in a while, since he's so far away."

A simple explanation.

And yet, *my* reaction to that was anything but simple.

That fear of falling fast and hard and deep dissipated. The love I felt grew, swelling like a balloon hooked up to a helium tank, getting bigger and bigger and *bigger*. Until I threatened to burst. He was looking after me in the only way he knew how. He was looking out for me by asking other people for help—which wasn't an easy thing for him to do. I *knew* that. And...truthfully, threaded through all of that was a tiny sliver of annoyance.

Just a little one.

He was meddling again.

He was taking care of me when I could take care of myself.

He was...

Loving me the only way he knew how.

So, I sucked in a breath, ignored the dirty look that Billie Rose was shooting Joel's way, and embraced Axel's love, no matter what form it came in.

"You guys want a beer?"

Twelve

AXEL

"Finnegan?"

I stopped in the hall, my messenger bag tossed over my shoulder, and glanced up in the direction of the slightly accented voice.

Pascal...I didn't actually know his last name.

Just...Pascal.

Like Madonna or Lizzo or Cher.

I forced myself to not smile at the thought. Mostly because that was going to split open the cut on my lip, and despite me considering myself a tough-ass hockey player, my little booboo on my bottom lip hurt, throbbing to my heartbeat.

Also, I didn't smile because I didn't think Pascal would appreciate the comparison to pop superstars.

But what did I know?

He might have a secret pop addiction and be out singing karaoke, finding his inner diva every time he disappeared into the shadows.

"Axel?" he asked, and I yanked myself out of my head.

Right. Less thoughts of pop divas and more focus on what the man was saying.

Pascal was the head of security for the Gold, and despite him having the impressive sneaking ability to appear and disappear seemingly out of thin air, at that exact moment, he was merely leaning against the wall, a duffle in his hand, no sneaking on display.

He tossed the bag to me. "The rest of your stuff."

I caught it. "Thanks, man."

"We checked out the hotel's camera feeds." A shake of his head. "She left after you did and didn't come back. No sign of her since that day, and a fake name on her application."

Damn.

I'd been hoping they could track down enough about her so that I could get a restraining order or at least a last name.

But no one seemed to know her.

Candi—yup, with an *i*—had spent lots of time in barrooms with my former teammates on the Rush—had spent a lot of time in *bed*rooms with them too. But no one knew her last name, and even Billie Rose didn't know exactly who she was, which was a surprise in itself.

She knew everyone from her town.

Which meant...Candi wasn't from River's Bend.

"We'll find her," Pascal said, clamping a hand onto my shoulder. "She won't get into any team facilities or events, I'll make sure of that. And I have some men checking leads in River's Bend."

Shock rippled through me. "I mean...that's really cool of you, but that's not really under the purview of the head of security of the Gold, right?" I shrugged. "I mean, so long as she doesn't come to my apartment or the rink or the arena...then the team doesn't really..."

"Care?"

Fuck.

Right, that sounded...dickish.

"No, it's not that—"

"You've got people you care about back home," Pascal said by way of explanation...which wasn't really an explanation, but it at least explained why he was looking into Candi and River's Bend. "I'll make sure they're safe so you can focus on things here."

"No offense, but..." I trailed off before I began to sound *dickish* again.

"Why do *I* care?" Pascal's lips tipped up just slightly at the edges.

Fuck.

More dickish.

I cleared my throat. "I—"

Pascal smirked. "I'm just fucking with you." Then he sobered. "I know what it's like to..." A pause that spoke of more than words. It spoke of pain and loss and—

Fuck if my long dead—and only recently reawakened heart— didn't twitch.

I hated the trap of feelings.

Or I had.

Before I fell in love.

But I hated that the trap of feelings opened me up to this situation, my heart going out to the other man.

Because I didn't know what to say.

I never did.

I hadn't grown up with empathy or sympathy or any -pathy.

My existence had always been...carve out every bit I could, hold tight like a dog protecting a bone, forget about everyone else.

Not in hockey.

Not at first.

But it had become that. Eventually, it had become that.

About me, about my misery, about wringing my time on the ice for every drop of pleasure it could produce.

About wringing that pleasure out of life and fuck everyone else's feelings.

Because *I* got what I needed.

Until handcuffs and pretty brown eyes and splinters in my ass. Until Brit and the players on the Gold had taken me under their wings. Until I'd realized all of what I was missing out on by living my life just for myself.

But that change didn't give me the right words to say to this man.

There *weren't* any *right* words for the kind of pain trapped in Pascal's dark brown eyes.

"...to be worried," Pascal finished quietly.

Firmly.

Putting a period on that part of the conversation before I had the chance to say *anything* of value.

"We'll find out her last name," he said. "And then I recommend filing a restraining order." A casual shrug of his shoulder. "Probably, won't dissuade her from approaching, but it will give you a paper trail in case things kick up again."

"Yeah," I said, my voice quiet. "That makes sense." I swallowed hard, scrambled for some words, for any fucking useful words. "Thank...uh...you for...um...putting the time in. I appreciate it."

Pascal glanced up at me, studied me closely.

Then he just squeezed my shoulder again...and disappeared.

I didn't know how the man did it, but one second he was there, and the next he was gone, and then I was staring at an empty hall like an idiot.

"Right," I whispered, knowing that I wouldn't discover Pascal's disappearing secret, not that day, probably not ever.

Shrugging, I continued out of the arena.

The night air hit my skin, cool and a little damp from the fog clinging to the sky, and I found myself sucking in a breath, soaking it in, something I never would have been able to do just months ago.

So maybe I didn't have all the right words.

Maybe I wouldn't *ever* have them.

But I'd also never been the kind of man to stand in the cool night air and *appreciate* it, to pause and even *notice* it.

So maybe I didn't have those words and maybe I'd spent my lifetime being a selfish asshole.

Maybe I wouldn't ever be perfect.

Maybe I wouldn't ever be good enough for Bailey.

But I was going to damn well try.

I inhaled that cool air, rolled my shoulders, and headed to my car.

Just as I gripped the driver's side handle, my cell rang.

Digging it out, I swiped and lifted it to my ear, listening to who was on the other end for just a couple of heartbeats before my lips turned up and warmth filled my belly as surely as the cool air clung to my skin.

This was the call I'd been waiting for.

Fucking *finally*.

THIRTEEN

BAILEY

The sun was just drifting over the hills to the east as I walked through my house.

Coffee was brewing, set to start on a timer before my alarm went off, thanks to the fancy new coffeemaker that Axel had bought for me.

It smelled glorious, helped clear the last of the cobwebs.

One would think after waking up this early for years—first during the summers with Gran and Gramps, and then after I'd taken on the ranch on my own, clawing it out of the financial black hole my parents had left it in—that I would be used to the early hour.

But every morning, I woke with crusty eyes and a foggy mind, and nothing cleared it until my first cup.

So, I headed straight for the kitchen, filled my mug.

Black, since I'd gotten used to it when I hadn't had the money to buy sugar and cream. Plus, the concentrated brew meant that the caffeine hit my bloodstream sooner and cleared all that fog out.

I blew on my cup until it was cool enough to drink and sucked down my elixir of life then quickly filled a travel mug so I could take it with me while I completed my morning chores. I was never hungry this early in the morning, so I didn't bother making anything, just grabbed my lined flannel jacket from the hooks by the front door and reached for the handle.

I couldn't lie and say that my heart didn't skip a beat every time I stepped out onto my porch, half expecting, half *wanting* there to be a hot, naked hockey player on the worn wooden planks.

Alas, that morning, it was empty of all naked, sexy hockey men.

It was empty of *everyone*.

Which was a good thing.

I didn't want to walk out and find my parents on the porch, or worse, Colt.

That had a shudder sliding down my spine, the cold morning sending me shivering, despite the belly full of coffee, despite my well-made flannel that could keep me warm even in the middle of winter—which, yeah, wasn't all *that* cold, since my Golden State blood was thin, but it didn't keep me warm.

Not that morning.

Probably not for a while yet.

Because...Colt.

He'd been on the farm.

He'd been in my house.

In my *house*. Maybe in my room.

Maybe touching my things.

I'd changed the sheets, bleached them, ran them twice through the water on the hottest cycle my washer could dish out.

And, even knowing it was in my head, I'd still thought that I'd caught a whiff of Colt's scent on them.

Impossible.

But...

"Enough," I whispered. Being stuck in the past was not what I needed this morning. Focus on the ranch, on my chores, on moving forward one foot at a time.

That was how I survived.

Plus, I'd woken up to a text message and a selfie from Axel, teasingly asking if I would still love him even with the fat lip and bruised nose.

I'd replied, even though he wouldn't see it until later, considering how late he normally fell asleep after games.

Sometimes, if I had a ton of shit to do on the ranch and had to get up early—or, well, had to get up for an earlier start than normal—he was just settling down from the adrenaline of the game and heading off to sleep.

We'd chat then as I was getting my coffee, as I walked across this empty porch, mug in hand.

Today, though, he didn't reply as I locked my front door—something I was doing every single time I left, even if it was just to go into the barn—and I was glad that he was sleeping, was getting some rest.

He was working hard.

I *wanted* him to rest.

Who was I?

Wanting to take care of a man when I promised that I would never trust my heart to one again.

But...my heart was safe with Axel.

I knew it.

I loved him, and at some point, I'd find the courage to tell him.

Soon.

Definitely soon.

Except...I didn't know if I'd really get there, if I'd be able to tell someone that again, to be *that* vulnerable and open and—

Actions were easier.

I could show him my love, show him without really putting myself out there.

"Coward," I muttered.

Sighing, I clomped down the stairs, walked along the path, and opened the door to the barn. Right now, I only had three horses inside—Data, and two others that were being boarded. Something I did to get extra money, and while I liked seeing the animals, it was something I was looking forward to stopping once I didn't need to scrimp and save and dig myself out of the hole my parents had dumped the ranch into.

I loved the horses.

I just wanted...less poop to clean up.

Grinning, I flicked on the lights, moved to Data's stall, and reached over to pet my baby's nose, feeling the soft huffs of her breath on my face.

She blew harder when I didn't immediately give her the apple I had in my pocket.

Something she knew I always had.

Thanks to Axel.

Which was another tick in his column, in the column of why I knew my heart was safe.

Because he noticed that I gave Data apples (and the occasional sugar cube because my horse was spoiled) and so there was always a supply of apples in my fridge and an airtight container of sugar cubes in the tack room.

Data huffed again, and I grinned, patting her nose one more time before stepping back and turning for the cutting board and knife I kept on a shelf nearby. "I need to slice this up, little miss," I said lightly. "As you well know." I plunked the apple down, lifted the knife, and...then nearly sliced my fucking finger off when a soft *"Moooo!"* radiated through the space.

Whirling, the knife dropping to the floor, I glanced at Data.

Who still had her head hanging over her stall door but hadn't suddenly gained the ability to make cow speak.

"Moooo!"

I jumped, thankfully without a sharp pointy thing in my hand this time.

"Moooo!"

"What the—?" I whirled from Data's stall trying to figure out—

"Moooo!"

There. The noise was coming from the far end of the barn, the stall that I always kept any orphaned or rejected cows in to get them big enough to rejoin the herd. It wasn't often, but occasionally a mama cow would give birth out of season and wouldn't take care of her calf and because I was...a soft touch, usually I stepped in.

Just like I'd stepped with—

"Moooo!"

"Picard," I whispered, seeing his adorable little head poking through a gap in the slats. My mouth fell open. "Picard?" I asked louder.

"Moooo!"

"What—I—" Then my feet were carrying me across the barn, and I was yanking at the stall door and—

There he was.

His gorgeous cow (calf? *steer?*) eyes on me and swear to fuck, it was almost like he was smiling at me, like he was happy to see me.

I'd sold him to the local petting zoo to pay for some expenses (namely, a cable package that meant I could see every game Axel played in), but hell if I hadn't shed a tear when I'd dropped Picard off. Yes, he was going to a good place with nice owners and kids who'd shower him with attention.

But Picard was *mine*.

I'd bottle-fed him for days, making sure he'd lived when it had been touch and go.

And—not that I'd admitted it to anyone—but I'd really missed him.

A *lot*.

"Oh, buddy," I whispered, skidding to a halt in front of the stall, dust and straw kicking up in all directions as I scrabbled with the door and yanked it open.

Then promptly found myself back on my ass, Picard clomping forward, dropping his head on my shoulder, and hell if he hadn't gotten bigger.

That was what animals did, I supposed.

Grow up.

I scratched behind his ears and tried not to be bowled over by his weight, laughing when he pressed his wet nose to my throat, mooing softly in my ear.

My cell rang, and I managed to drag it out of my pocket.

Axel.

Of course it was him.

I swiped, put it up to my ear.

"Hey, buttercup."

My heart knew it was safe.

Emotion danced in my veins.

Bubbled up in my throat.

And the words just rolled right off my tongue.

"I love you."

FOURTEEN

AXEL

I was in bed with the blankets around my waist, counting the minutes after I'd gotten her text trying to guesstimate how long it would take her to get to the barn, to see what I'd managed to set up last night.

Thanks to Billie Rose.

And an obscene donation to the petting zoo that Bailey had sold the cow to.

They'd better put my name on a plaque somewhere.

Smirking, I hit her name in my contacts, listened as it rang through.

"Hey, buttercup," I said when she answered.

"I love you."

Shock ricocheted through me, stronger than a check from that fucker on the Breakers. Conner something. Smith.

That was right.

Smitty, his teammates called him.

That fucker could hit like a Mack truck.

But he had nothing on those words.

They flew through the airwaves, collided with my eardrums, and—

I dropped my cell.

Then I heard them in my mind again, her soft and gentle voice telling me she loved me. She *loved* me.

And suddenly I was a flurry of motion, scrambling for my cell, trying to grab it again, trying to find it in the blankets which had somehow seemed to multiply into a fucking dumpster's worth of fabric. I could hear Bailey's voice faintly coming through the speakers.

Fuck.

She'd just given me something big, and for all she knew, I was disavowing it by not answering, by cutting off the call.

I was an idiot.

I had a voice. I could hear hers, so clearly she'd be able to hear mine. I just needed...to fucking *use* it.

"Bailey—Bailey, I'm here," I said, still scrambling. *Fuck. Where was my phone?* "I'm here and I love you, too and—" A glimpse of black, the edge of my phone case. I snatched it and— "Bailey? Bailey? Did you hear me? I love you, too. I love you so much."

Finally, I got the cell up to my ear.

And was greeted by laughter.

Ah. Romance.

"Really, buttercup?" It was a snapped-out question. It was totally not the right tone for this moment.

More laughter.

"Oh God," she gasped, the air crackling through the speakers, hitting my ears. "This is too perfect. We started with splinters in your ass and a saw near your femoral, and now I'm making you scramble by declaring my love for you."

I growled. "I didn't scramble."

"Oh, so that noise I was hearing was you just lying in bed relaxing?"

"You're a pain in my ass."

"I'm *your* pain in the ass."

I growled again but didn't answer. Because it was true.

She was mine. *Mine.*

"One you love, too," she added softly.

My lungs went a little tight with that, all the emotion in my veins going taut as I warred with the need to protect myself, to lock everything down and hold it tight, to get my slice and keep it for me, me, *me.*

But...I loved her.

So, I didn't argue, just whispered, "Buttercup."

She laughed softly. "We're a pair, aren't we?"

I clenched my cell, pressed it harder to my ear. "Yeah," I whispered. "We are."

"So scared of love and attachment that Billie Rose had to get involved."

That had me relaxing, my laughter joining hers. "Fucking Billie Rose," I grumbled.

A pause then, "Worth all her interference though, huh?"

I thought of Bailey's aunt, the mayor of River's Bend, and the fact that she'd been there for Bailey time and again, had stepped up again, just the night before to help me smuggle Picard home, and I smiled. "Definitely worth it, buttercup."

My voice had gentled in a way it never would have before.

Because I loved this woman.

"I'm guessing you found him?"

"Him?" A beat of amusement before she changed the call to video, showing me a feed of her...and the cow I'd bought from the petting zoo that had practically crawled into her lap. "Oh, you mean Picard?" She rubbed the cow's neck, tone going babyish. "Aren't you just the sweetest little boy," she crooned. "You're the best boy. The best cow-boy ever."

"Cow-boy?" I teased.

Her eyes hit mine through the video. "Really?"

"I mean, I'm not the one who's going all gaga over a cow-boy."

God, I missed her. If she was there with me, I could have pulled her into my arms, could have held her as I teased her, kissed away her annoyance.

Could have kissed something else.

"He's a steer," she said icily, propping the cell on the stall door and wrapping her arms around him.

"Named Picard."

"And you're not even here for me to smack away your teasing."

"Is that *smacking* in the way I hope?"

She frowned. "What—"

I waggled my brows.

Her face went slack. "Really?" she asked dryly.

I grinned. "Don't tell me you haven't been thinking about me touching that ass, me squeezing and smacking and *taking* it."

Her lips parted, pink on her cheeks. "Damn you, Finnegan."

"What?" I asked innocently.

"You're turning me on in front of my—"

"*Moooo!*"

"—cow-son," she finished.

And now I was laughing again, and she was too, and then her face was going serious. "Axel?"

"Yeah, honey?"

"You really did this for me?" The question was a little damp and that hit me. Hard.

"What?" I asked lightly. "Paid to get your cow-boy-son back or because now I owe Billie Rose a favor for helping me smuggle Picard in?"

"I love you," she whispered. "You know that, right?"

"I know that. And"—it was different saying it when I could see her face, her eyes, her soft, soft expression—"you know I love you, too."

A long pause.

"Terrifying saying that aloud, isn't it?" she whispered.

I sucked in a breath. "Buttercup."

"But you know how I know it's right?"

I shook my head.

"Because of—"

"*Moooo!*"

She stilled.

Then burst out laughing.

"Because of moos," she said once she'd gotten control of herself, "and carpet in my house, food in my fridge, text messages I wake up to"—her lips turned up—"even sad-eyed selfies with swollen lips I want to kiss. I'm terrified, scared out of my fucking mind to love you, but I also know there's no other choice. You're mine."

Fuck if my eyes didn't sting as those words settled deep.

"I wish I was there," I murmured.

"For ass play?"

That was so far from what I'd expected that I felt my mouth drop open, felt it flop like a fish for a few moments.

Then I remembered that I was Axel Finnegan.

Bailey might make me feel like I could be someone else, someone else down to my very core, but I still was me.

And that meant I had bravado. I had snark.

I smirked at her.

"I'm looking forward to seeing that ass the next time I'm home." A beat. "To taking that ass."

Her lips parted, that pink coming back.

"I seem to remember you saying you could resist my smolder," I teased.

A smile, and I knew she was probably remembering the same thing I had. Being in that barn, our bodies close, the attraction tugging us together even as we were desperate to stay apart. I expected sass in return, expected her to be sharp back.

But instead, I got soft.

I got Bailey.

And it reminded me why she owned me.

"I could never resist you, Axel Finnegan," she murmured. "Now go to bed," she ordered. "I have chores to do."

"Okay, buttercup," I said, scooting down in bed, fatigue wrapping loosely around my ankles, ready to tug me into oblivion. "Whatever you say."

"What if I say that I want you to take my ass, too?"

My eyes shot wide.

Sleep was forgotten.

She smirked.

"Sweet dreams, honey."

"Wait—"

She hung up.

And I...

Well, sleep was a long time coming...mostly because my fingers wrapped around my cock and I stroked hard and fast...and dreamed about seeing that smirk in person.

And that ass.

Fifteen

Bailey

Well, I'd said it.
   I hadn't meant to.
   And...
He'd said it back.

I pressed a hand to my heart.

It still thudded against my ribs, my palms were still slick, and my legs...sweet baby Jesus, they trembled when I went to stand.

Like I'd just reached the end of the biggest adrenaline letdown. Ever. And it had left me nearly unable to stand.

"*Moooo!*"

Picard bumped me, and he was so big that he nearly knocked me over.

"*Neigh.*"

I grinned. Clearly, Data wasn't happy about the delay in her morning apple. "Coming, baby," I called, and sucked in a breath, tucking my romantic heart down, *way* down. Then I left Picard's stall door open since he would follow me around like a little puppy.

Not so little anymore.

But he still did follow me around.

First to the shelf.

Where I finally cut up Data's apple and then made a pit stop for a sugar cube since she'd been so patient through my phone call and Picard love fest.

She huffed indignantly, but accepted my offering, and then I moved around the barn, refilling water and feed buckets, putting my pair of boarders out into separate paddocks since they couldn't be trusted to get along.

Shoveling, raking, sweeping—the part of this job that kept me most in shape.

Then I tucked Picard back into his stall, knowing he would be ready for some food and rest and would be content while I went out on Data to check on the fences and the herd.

Data danced a bit when I settled her saddle on top of her, cinching it tight, but it wasn't because she was unhappy. She was impatient, ready to have her head, ready to go galloping through the foothills, and okay, maybe a *little* unhappy that her run had been delayed by Picard.

I slipped her another sugar cube.

She huffed in approval.

Then I finished with the reins, led her out, and mounted up, and I...rode.

Fuck, it was the best feeling outside of an orgasm.

It was almost the same, the pleasure and joy, the oblivion and how it pulled me from my head. The way it exploded from my middle and filled every part of my body.

It should be part of the job.

It was something I did for hours, almost every day.

But...it wasn't pedestrian. *Never* did riding Data feel pedestrian.

This was...freedom.

The thud of Data's hooves, the wind against my skin, through my hair, the hiss of the grass waving in the air, the chirps of birds, the *moos* in the distance. A quiet place, and yet full of so much noise that I never failed to notice something different.

Though, that morning, it was a stretch of fence down.

That wasn't different, I supposed.

The fencing was old and I'd gotten around to replacing a lot of it, but the elements were rough, and I'd often had to scrape together the materials. Which meant that they didn't last as long as they should or as long as I wanted.

This stretch I'd done right around the time I'd taken over the ranch.

And now the half-rotted posts had given away.

Sighing, I made a mental note of its location, moved on to survey any further problems, and made sure the water troughs were clean and full.

Then Data and I were heading in, my fun done, the real work ahead.

The other horses—Sam and Frodo—needed their rides. Hay had to be brought out on the UTV, since there wasn't enough grass left at this point in the year for the entire herd to graze and get enough nutrients from it.

I wanted them fat and happy before I sold them off.

First, I used the UTV—and the hay on its back—to tempt a few heifers who'd decided to go rogue on me through the broken stretch of fence. Then I sorted the downed posts, restrung the barbed wire between them and made sure there would be no further runaways, at least through *that* section of fencing.

Then I dropped the rest of the hay in a few separate spots and headed back in to take care of Sam and Frodo.

Unfortunately, I wasn't alone on the ranch.

There was a car in the driveway, and I knew who it belonged to.

And as I drove in, I debated just driving by and moving

straight to town. Except that would leave my ex too fucking close to Data, to Picard, and Christ almighty, I couldn't have that.

And...I wasn't that woman anymore.

I was stronger, had been forged in steel and fire.

And I...wasn't alone.

Slowing before I reached the driveway, I typed out a text to Billie Rose, letting her know that Colt was there.

And...then I blew out a breath and drove the rest of the way.

Colt opened the door.

The fear was...overwhelming, intense, but I breathed through it, or at least I pulled up my big girl panties and decided that I was going to *brazen* my way through it.

I stopped the UTV outside of the barn, not wanting to be closed in if he got close.

And he would probably get close.

He moved toward me, eyes cold in that way I'd always thought were warm. But I knew now that the warmth was actually a façade.

Beneath was a coiled rattled snake with venom-tipped fangs.

"That's close enough," I said when he'd begun to move around the UTV.

He didn't stop. *Of course* he didn't.

He rounded the hood and closed the distance between us.

My fingers closed around the cold metal barrel, just as he said, "Baby."

I lifted the shotgun out of the rack on the back of the UTV, turned—

And pointed it to the center of Colt's chest.

"That's. Close. *Enough,"* I growled.

Amusement in his dark brown eyes, cold and barbed and sharp enough to wound. "Baby," he said again, the condescension so heavy that it nearly knocked me to my feet.

I locked my knees, lifted my chin. "I said—"

He jerked forward, the movement so fast that my eyes couldn't track it.

But my body did.

My body was familiar with those sharp, jerking movements of his, and it had a deep-buried instinct to protect itself from this man.

So even before he could touch me with that brutal, horrible hand, I was already scrambling back, already putting distance between us.

And my finger was already...

Closing around the trigger.

Sixteen

Axel

"So," Olivia said, "what are we going to do with that pretty boy face of yours?"

My agent was pretty.

My agent was *gorgeous*, actually.

My agent was a shark, recommended by Brit, who wore six-inch heels and bright red lipstick and...a suit that showed off every inch of her baby belly.

I slouched back in the visitors' chair, stared at her, the wide wooden expanse between us. "I like to think of it as a pretty *manly* face."

Her lips tipped up. "Po-tay-to. Po-tah-toe." Then she reached for some papers, passed them over, tone going businesslike. "It's always good to plan for a career after hockey. Hopefully, you'll have a long time in the league"—a smile—"but hockey is a dangerous sport, so I like to plan for other eventualities."

That seemed logical.

That seemed responsible.

Planning for a life after hockey.

Except—

"Planning isn't really something I do a lot of."

Now, her smile widened. "That's why I do the job *I* do, and you do the job *you* do."

"Brit was right."

"That I'm a badass?" Olivia quipped, buffing her knuckles on her shoulder. "Damn right."

I folded my hands over my middle. "No, though that's true also. She was right that you guys are the best." And that my previous agent had been shit.

Though, I was working on my diplomacy skills.

So, I just thought the last and left the rest to her imagination.

"Yeah, well," she said. "I don't know if you'll be saying the same for me when I've got you modeling underwear."

I shrugged. "I'm down with modeling underwear."

"I—" Her eyes went wide. "What?"

"I've spent more than my fair share of time being naked." Another shrug. "Actually wearing clothes—even underwear— would be a nice change of pace."

Now *she* sat back, smiling again. "I think you're going to be my favorite client. All the rest of them"—she waved a hand—"get so shy about showing off their moneymakers."

Money.

Right.

That was another good point.

Money I could use to help Bailey with the ranch. Money I could use to get her some help, give her some freedom so that she could get her teaching credentials, do something that wasn't ranching, wasn't her dream.

"How much can I make modeling?" I asked.

"Depends," she said, nodding toward the papers.

I scrolled through the stack, reading through the summary she'd Post-It-Noted to the front of each contract. That was...

That was a lot of money.

Even the ones with less money still offered more money than I'd seen since I signed my Gold contract...and there were *a lot* of them. I could...I could do a lot with this money.

"Okay," I said, glancing up.

"Okay?"

"I'll do them. All or whichever ones you think are best." I set the papers on the desk, leaned back in the chair.

"All?"

"I'm down. I don't have kids or a wife. I've got a girlfriend who's four hours away and a loaner apartment. I want her here. I want roots. So, I'll do what you advise, and I'll bank that shit so that when I'm done on the rink, I can give my woman a good life."

She lifted one black brow. "I thought you said she was just a girlfriend."

Yeah, girlfriend didn't really encompass everything.

Didn't encompass *anything* about how I felt.

"I meant that she's my forever."

For a second, Olivia's brash, tough exterior faded, her expression going gentle. "I know something about forever." She pointed to her belly. "Which is why the first contract I'll ask you to take is the most selfish one—and the one with the smallest paycheck."

Frowning, I just lifted my brows and waited.

"Cole"—her husband and a former NHL player—"has a charity. It brings city kids to the outdoors—kayaking, horseback riding, camping, s'mores, anything they might not have when they're stuck in a place with lots of tall buildings and limited green space. They need someone to model their merch, but they can't afford any big names, and Cole will do a lot for the camp, but he won't do that."

"Okay," I agreed.

Her brows lifted. "Just like that?"

"It helps us both—" And shit, was I seriously, without a single second thought, willing to do something for someone without it solely benefitting me and just me?

I paused.

Breathed.

Yeah. I fucking was.

Miracles happened, I supposed.

Or maybe I was just growing up.

"My woman has a cattle ranch up in the Sierra foothills," I said. "It's a lot for her to manage." I shrugged. "I want to help her."

"A bigger contract would make more sense then," Olivia countered.

"Probably," I agreed. "But I've also seen her face when she comes back from a ride. There's something magical out there for her."

Olivia blinked.

"And the kids deserve to find that too," I finished, feeling a bit dopey, but glad I got the words out anyway.

Olivia paused, studying him closely. "I thought you were supposed to be an asshole."

Laughter bubbled through me. "Oh, I am."

She began flipping through papers, pulled open a drawer, closed it. Opened another.

"What are you doing?" he asked after a moment, frowning.

"Looking for your assholeness."

Said without the slightest bit of hesitation.

Fuck she was funny.

Kind of like another woman I knew.

"Is it next to your lipstick?"

Her head shot up, her mouth, painted that bright red, twisted up. "There it is."

"My assholeness?"

"Yup."

I laughed again. Then shook my head and focused, even though part of me felt like I could banter with her all day. "I'll do the merch," I said. "And then the rest of them."

Her eyes gleamed and she reclined in her chair, back to business. "I think I'm going to love working with you. A perfectly moldable block of clay."

"I can't decide if that's an insult or a compliment."

Her head tilted from side to side. "Maybe a little of both?"

"Fuck," I said, laughing. "Give it to me straight, why don't you?"

"Always," she said and her tone was serious enough that I felt that word like a vow.

So I made the same back with a nod.

"If your woman wants to come out to the ranch," she offered, "I'm sure Cole would love to talk shop."

Now *that* got me excited. Bailey would love that. "Let's make it happen."

"See?" A beatific smile. "You like me."

I grinned and then because I was me, I added, "My bank account likes you."

"Asshole." A smirk. "But mine likes you for the same reason."

"I—"

My cell rang, and normally I wouldn't have answered it, but it was Bailey's ringtone. "Sorry," I told Olivia. "I need to take—"

"Take it." She stood. "I'll give you some privacy." She started to move toward the door, hand going to the knob, ready to close it behind her as I answered the call.

"Buttercup—"

"Oh fuck, Axel," she said. "Oh fuck, I— Oh fuck, oh fuck, oh *fuck!*"

SEVENTEEN

BAILEY

My finger closed around the trigger.

Colt smirked, bending close until the barrel pressed right against the center of his chest.

My finger tightened.

"Back up."

It wasn't strong. It was breathless, bordering on begging.

And he knew it.

He knew he could do that to me again.

Could hurt me and I couldn't stop him and—

My finger rested on that small piece of curved metal.

"Baby," he said in that frozen silken tone. "I came all this way to see you."

Fingers wrapped in my hair, yanking so that my scalp burned, chunks being ripped free.

Fists connecting with my ribs, a boot with my side.

Rain pelting down on my body, my clothes soaked through and chilling me to the bone. My hair plastered to my skull, my scalp burning from the frigid downpour, from the pain this man had borne on me.

The memories cleared.

I breathed.

"I want you to go," I said, stronger now.

But still not strong enough.

He leaned in, pushed against the barrel, and I had to brace myself so that I didn't fall back. "But if I went, if I stayed away..." He ran a finger over the cylinder of metal. "Then I wouldn't get what I want."

The smooth metallic trigger was still cool beneath my finger. "You won't get anything from me, not ever again," I vowed.

His arm came up like a shot, hand streaking toward my cheek.

I flinched, but when he touched me, my finger didn't tighten, it didn't do anything but stay there on that trigger, resting limp against the crescent-shaped metal.

Cold crept up my toes, gripped my ankles, anchored me in place when I should have run. *Run.*

Back in the UTV.

Back away from this man.

I managed a half step in retreat.

"Aren't you going to ask?" he asked, the words a dagger's point.

"Wh-what?"

"Aren't you going to ask what I want?" he asked silkily.

Dangerously.

No. I wasn't. I couldn't. Not after all of this time. After all the work I'd done to get better, to forget, to move on and not be this frightened cowering woman. I *couldn't*—

Finally, there was steel in me.

Steel that had my knees going steady, steel that forged my spine into a stiff, metal spike.

Steel that ordered him to "Back up."

Colt cocked his head to the side. "Don't you remember?" he

whispered. "Don't you remember how much I enjoyed sucking the fight out of you?"

That steel went cold, threatened to shatter, threatened to send me to the gravel.

But I lifted my chin, held on. "I remember," I said. "But that was then."

His mouth turned up. "If you give me what I want then I won't have to hurt you *now*."

My finger tightened.

"Back. Up."

A smirk. "You won't shoot me."

"I will," I gritted out. "I'll kill you if you touch me again."

He was close in an instant, fingers grazing my cheek.

Almost gently.

But he was Colt, so they were a threat and ultimately not gentle, not really. They were a soft promise of violence.

I just didn't understand why he was here, why he was here *now*.

A noise sounded behind me, but I didn't dare look, didn't do anything except caress the metal trigger.

"Back. Up."

The noise grew.

I knew it was soft. I knew that unless someone had spent summers on this ranch, had spent several lonely years since, the quiet cocooning all around them, they wouldn't recognize it.

Knew that Colt wouldn't understand what it meant.

But I did.

The shotgun still pointed at his chest, I took another step back.

"I want this ranch, baby," he said, leaning toward me. "I want the land and the cattle and that sweet little setup of that house."

No.

That wasn't going to happen.

Not ever.

"I don't give a fuck what you want," I said and it was strong now, a fierce snap of words. "That's not happening. Now go or I'll call—"

"Who?" he sneered. "I don't see your man around." He threw a hand out in the direction of the barn then the house. "And you're certainly not going to shoot me."

Axel wasn't around.

And wouldn't be around much. Not until the season was over.

But still...I wasn't alone.

Remembering that was why I had kept the picture—the wedding picture of me and Colt. Why I had left it exactly where Gramps had first placed it years ago, why I hadn't torn it to shreds and thrown it away when I'd moved in. It was for *this* moment, when the memories were swirling, the *fear* had sunk itself deep. *This* was why I held tight to the reminder of what life could be like, what *I* could be like under the wrong circumstances.

Not alone.

Not any longer.

Not that woman.

Not ever again.

"I don't need a man around. I have myself. I have my friends. And yes, I have Axel. But more than that, even when I'm by myself, I am"—my eyes flicked to the side as the sound of gravel crunching seemed to finally reach him—"*not* alone."

His eyes narrowed. "I'm not going to stop until I get what I want."

"You'll never get what you want from me," I whispered.

Sparks of fury in his gaze, a muscle in his jaw flexing, and then, quick as a snake, he cocked his fist back.

He was going to hit me.

Hard.

With that tight fist.

And I didn't think.

I didn't *think.*

My finger just tightened around the trigger, tightened and tightened and *tightened* until…

The shotgun went off.

———

I screamed.

Or maybe that was Colt.

Or maybe it was just all in my head.

But as I tried to process that, the gun was snatched out of my hands, and I was yanked back and—

"Steady now," the male voice said. "I have you."

And then my eyes were opening, and I was staring at a broad back.

At *Joel's* broad back.

And I started trembling.

"Easy," he said, and the arm that had wrapped around my middle tensed, pressing me into his back. "I'm here—"

"You could have killed me, you fucking madwoman!"

Colt.

I burrowed into Joel, and he gave me one more squeeze before dropping his arm.

"You invited onto this property?"

It was a rumbled question, and a deadly one.

"I—how dare—"

"He wasn't," I whispered. "I asked him to go, again and *again*."

Joel went even more tense, even more still. Even more deadly. "She asked you to go?"

Another dangerous query.

"She doesn't know what she wants," Colt snapped.

"But she *did* want to be hit?" Joel asked coldy, telling me that he'd seen Colt wind up, that he wasn't made at me for taking the shot.

That his anger at my ex was an icicle perched on the ceiling, ready to fall.

To pierce.

To kill.

"No," I said, my shock having worn off. "I didn't want to be hurt. To be *hit*." I slid slightly to the side, moved so that I could see Colt, see that he was unharmed.

Mostly.

A series of holes had been left in the ground, rocks and dirt dispersed by the blast. They must have ricocheted up because there was blood dripping down his legs from the ricochet of the bird shot.

But he was otherwise unhurt.

I hadn't killed him.

I'd wanted to—*wanted* to so fucking badly.

But at the last minute, I'd aimed at the ground anyway.

And now I realized that my legs stung as well.

"I didn't want to be hurt," I said again, leaning against Joel, taking strength from him when I hardly knew him, except that Axel had sent him and if Axel had been here he would have let me do the same—

"I didn't want to be hurt *then*, and I didn't want to be hurt now." I straightened slightly. "I want you to go, to get the fuck out of my life." I swallowed hard. "I want you to get out and never come back."

Colt's eyes flashed and he took a step toward us. "You don't get to—"

Joel moved.

One second he was next to me.

The next he had Colt's shirt in his grip and was shoving my ex back, step by step by *step*.

Until they were at his car.

Until Joel had him pressed up against the middle and then said something that had Colt going pale, his fingers scrabbling for the handle, yanking open the door, and wrestling himself from Joel's hold.

Or maybe Joel let him go.

I didn't know.

I only watched as Colt slammed the door, tore out of the driveway, rocks skittering in all directions.

And then Joel was back in front of me, hands on my shoulders. "Bailey—"

We both turned to the sound of another car coming down the drive, and I saw that it was Billie Rose's.

The next moment she was skidding to a halt.

But before she got out of her car, Joel reached into the UTV and handed me my cell. "Call Axel. I'll handle that harpy."

Probably, I should be insulted for my aunt's honor.

Except I was shaking.

Trembling so hard that I had a tough time holding my phone.

"Call him," he repeated, squeezing my fingers around my cell. "He'll make it better."

I sucked in a breath.

But he was gone, moving toward Billie Rose, stopping her when she would have run toward me.

And...finally.

I got my fingers to move.

To dial.

EIGHTEEN

AXEL

"You can't keep doing this," she whispered.

The moment I'd gotten the phone call, I'd driven like a bat out of hell.

Making the four-hour drive in just over three hours.

Too fucking long.

Too many things that could have gone wrong, too easily.

But I was here now.

Holding Bailey, in her bed, and trying to figure out how in the fuck to get away with murder.

That bastard had come to the ranch, had gotten in Bailey's face, could have so easily hurt her if Joel hadn't already been on his way to the ranch. If Billie Rose hadn't gotten Bailey's text and, because she wasn't close, had called Joel, finding out where he was and telling him to hurry.

Lucky.

So fucking lucky.

"How are your legs?" I whispered, smoothing my hand down her thigh.

She was wearing sweatpants, so I couldn't get a look at the bandages I'd painstakingly placed that afternoon. Small cuts on her shins, her ankles.

"I told you they're fine."

"Buttercup."

"Look," she said, sitting up. Her tone was stern, though there was soft in her eyes. "I...appreciate that you want to protect me, but—"

"You're *fine?*"

That phone call had been...

"Joel forced me to call you then." She shook her head. "I shouldn't have. Not right then."

That...

Stung.

Fucking hell, it stung.

"I love you," I said. "I should have been here and—"

She cursed and pulled out of my grip, pushed out of bed. "And I love you, too. And I don't want to be a fucking distraction, a fucking *burden*. Maybe..." She pushed her hair out of her face. "Maybe we should stop seeing each other."

The sound that rose in my throat was animalistic.

A raw, inhuman sound of pain.

"Just until after the season is over," she added quickly. "This has all moved so fast, and it's a lot, and you're in San Francisco. You're trying to live out your dream, honey. I-I can't be the reason you don't get—"

I was moving before I realized my feet had carried me across the room.

"Why do you think I'm where I am?" I snapped, throwing out a hand, hating that she winced at the abrupt movement, hating that her *ex* had made it so *that* was her reaction when I got a little heated. I took a breath, gentled my voice, slowed my movements despite the blood pumping through my body, demanding that I end this conversation with her here and now before it...before it damaged something between us. "If it weren't for you, if it weren't for what we found together, what we've *shared* together, I'd still be here in town, fucking and drinking and sitting in my misery."

She didn't respond, just looked away, was quiet for a long time.

Then she turned back and her mouth opened and I knew, *knew* that she was going to spew some fucking bullshit. "What we have isn't—"

I pressed a finger to her lips. "Don't," I whispered or begged or—

"Don't what?" she asked against my skin.

"Don't take what we have and ruin it."

Her eyes slid closed. Her body went still.

And slowly, oh so slowly, I wrapped my arms around her and held her against me.

My heart was a fucking drum in my chest, my body demanded that I carry her back into bed, that I fuck her until she was limp and satiated, until she wouldn't dream of leaving me.

But...I wanted more with Bailey.

I wanted forever.

When she remained silent, I didn't relax. We seemed to be on a precipice, and one word from her, one sentiment that this didn't mean as much to her as it did to me, would send me over the edge, tumbling down to the gully below, sharp rocks ready to impale me, heavy ones overhead ready to break off, fall, and crush me.

Eventually, though, she nodded, dropping her head to my chest, her body slumping against mine. "I'm used to taking care of myself."

"I know."

"I was scared today. Really scared." A pause, long and taut and *painful.* "I hate that he still scares me."

"He hurt you. Even the simplest of animals avoid pain."

"He *took* me..." A sigh. "He took me away from myself, turned me into someone I didn't recognize. And he did it today, too. At least for a little bit." Her voice dropped to a whisper. "I don't want to go back there. I don't want to be that woman."

"I know."

Her head tilted back, eyes on mine. "No blanket assurances that I won't ever be that woman again?"

I cupped her cheek. God, I wish I could. I *wanted* to. But I wouldn't lie to her.

I couldn't.

"I don't think anyone can make them. Not with one hundred percent certainty anyway."

Teeth pressing to her bottom lip, but then she sighed again, and then eventually...she nodded. "No," she agreed. "No one can."

"But I believe in the woman who stood up to me, who stood up to *him*. I know she has an inner strength that I envy, that I *respect*, and because of that, I have faith that she'll never go back. Because she—" I smoothed my knuckles over her cheek. "Because *you've* come far, buttercup. And I don't think you'll allow yourself to do anything but to keep inching forward."

"Axel," she whispered, her head dropping forward again, resting against my chest.

"Buttercup."

She shuddered.

"I'm sorry," she whispered.

"I know. And I love that you would try to protect me, but—"

A sigh. "We're not like that." She lifted her head, met my gaze, and her mouth turned up. "We're just two broken people who found each other."

My lips twitched, but I drew her closer, pressed my body to hers. "I know something that *isn't* broken."

"Yeah?"

I nipped the tip of her nose. "Yeah."

"What might that be?"

"Besides my cock desperate for your ass?"

She laughed. "Such sweet, romantic words."

"One of these days, I'll tempt you into it."

Her hand slid down my chest, flitted under the hem of my T-shirt. She rose on tiptoe, mouth finding my earlobe, sucking lightly. "For the record, you won't have to do much to tempt me into it."

Grinning, I smoothed my hand over the ass in question. "Yeah?"

A kiss to my jaw. "I've enjoyed everything you've ever done to me." To my cheek. "I don't suspect you'll ever do anything I don't like."

I wouldn't.

I'd make it my mission to give her only pleasure. Never pain. She'd had too much pain in her life already.

"I wouldn't."

"I know that." Conviction in each word that settled deep in my heart.

"Yeah?" I asked again.

She tsked. "Don't get rid of my filthy puckboy, not *now*."

"Why not *now*?"

A kiss to my jaw. "Because I like him." A kiss to the corner of my mouth. "I like you." A beat. "*All* of you."

"Yeah?"

She grinned, and her fingers dipped under the waistband of my pants. "Yeah, honey."

NINETEEN

A xel had left around nine the night before, needing to get back into town so he was fresh for the game today.

I'd waited up until I'd gotten his text that he'd arrived at his apartment

And now I'd wandered into my kitchen only to find a note.

There should be a delivery on your porch by the time you
wake up.
-A
P.S. He's safe. But call me if you need confirmation.

"He's?" I muttered.

But the note didn't bring me any further answers, and neither did my phone.

No illuminating text messages.

No additional post-scripts on the back of the note.

Frowning, I screwed the top on my to-go carafe, grabbed my flannel, and headed to the door, my boots clomping on the floor.

Joel couldn't possibly be out there.

He'd had to get on the bus to an away game yesterday after-noon, and he and his fellow Rush players wouldn't be back for several days.

And Axel was, obviously back in San Francisco.

I turned the handle, cracked open the door, and—

Gasped.

"Oh my God," I squealed, moving forward to the crate, to the adorable ball of fluff—gray and white with black spots and—

"Oh my God," I squealed again.

And two different colored eyes—one a light brown, one a pale blue.

"An Australian Shepherd," a lightly accented voice said from the shadows.

I jumped, squealing for a third time, though this time it didn't have anything to do with puppies and their adorableness. It had to do with a strange man on my porch, one who seemed to magically appear out of the shadows.

"Pascal," he said. "Head of security for the Gold."

I frowned. "Long way from home, Pascal." Then I lifted my cell and called Axel. I hated to wake him, but...was the delivery the dog, the man, or both?

"Buttercup," Axel answered on the first ring.

"The man or the dog?"

"Both," he responded without hesitation. "Pascal owns a secu-rity firm in addition to his work with the Gold. He was in town looking into Candi for me. He's going to take over from Joel to keep an eye on the ranch until he can get someone to stay there with you."

"What?"

"Just until we sort out your parents and Colt," he added in a hurry. "Or the season's over and I can stay there."

"The season? Axel? I can't ask—"

"You didn't ask," he said, still hurrying.

How much did live-in security cost?

More than I could afford, certainly.

"It's too much money—"

"Nothing is too much to make sure you're safe."

Fuck. That had my heart going all squirmy.

"I'm doing this, honey."

I sucked in a breath.

"You're not that woman from the picture anymore, not the woman from your nightmares."

I released that breath.

"You're not alone, buttercup," he said softly. "Which means that you have me, you have friends. You just need to accept the help."

"You've done so much for me already. I can't—"

"It'll give me peace of mind so I can play better," he countered.

I sighed, clenched the phone tightly. "You already used that line on me."

A pause. "I don't recall that conversation," he teased.

I snorted, pressed the cell to my ear, keeping it in place by lifting my shoulder as I bent to scoop up the puppy. "*Right.*"

"Nope." A pop on the p. "Don't recall it at all."

"I accepted the house stuff," I pointed out.

"So, you'll accept this, too?" A hopeful question.

I sighed, stroked my hand down the puppy's back, feeling my fingers sink into the soft fur. "*Axel.*"

"Please, buttercup?" he asked, sounding truly pathetic, though laughter bubbled up in me when he added, "Just saying, if we were on a video call right now, I would be giving you sad puppy eyes."

"Which is the perfect segue for the ball of fluff currently giving *me* sad puppy eyes?"

"You like him?"

I already *loved* him. "He's adorable."

"Australian Shepherds are working dogs—*herding* dogs," Axel said. "He can help you on the ranch, and they're protective as well."

"Fuck," I whispered as his words flowed through me, made my heart skip a beat.

"What?" he asked softly.

"Why are you doing this to me?"

To his credit, he didn't need to ask me if I was being serious. He knew I was, but he knew also exactly what I meant.

And how *I* knew this?

Because his response was, "Loving you?"

"Yeah," I whispered. "Exactly that."

"File a police report, okay?"

"I already did that yesterday. Frank is going to fast-track a restraining order."

"Good, honey."

The puppy glanced up and yawned and I had to bite back a giggle. Then I couldn't hold back my laughter when he put his paws on my shoulders and licked my chin. "Yeah. It is good."

Axel.

The pup.

Joel and Pascal, who was standing, his back against the railing, eyes on me, face placid, but not impatient, not cold.

He was dangerous.

Anyone could see that with a single glance at the man.

But he wasn't dangerous to *me*.

He wasn't like Colt.

I felt that in my bones.

Because of that, I glanced back down at the pup just as Axel spoke again. "What are you going to name him? Spock?" A beat. "Or Wish Bear?"

"God, I hate that you know all my secrets," I grumbled.

"Not *all* of them."

I sucked in a breath. "No," I agreed.

"But I will."

The air hissed out of my lungs. I took another breath, released it slowly, and admitted the truth, "Yes." A beat. "But only because I know you'll share all your secrets, too."

"Yeah, buttercup. I will."

I laughed softly.

"What?" he asked.

"I want to tell you that I love you, but I can't abide by the fact that I'm turning into a sappy asshole."

"You're not an asshole. That's my job, remember?"

"Yeah," I said, thinking of our rocky start, "I remember."

"Ouch, honey." But I knew he was in his bed, knew he was smiling, knew he loved me, knew he loved when I sassed him. "Spock, yeah?" he said. "To continue the theme."

My heart. My *heart*.

It couldn't survive Axel Finnegan.

But still, I said, "Yeah honey, I think you're right." A breath, shaking off the sap. "Now, go back to bed. I've got chores to do and apparently, a puppy to train."

"There are supplies in the barn. A crate and beds and food."

Of course he'd thought of that, even before I'd managed to put together that I would need to take a trip into town for supplies.

I couldn't survive Axel Finnegan.

I couldn't.

But it'd be the best sort of death.

"Now, I really do have to tell you that I love you," I said.

I could hear the smile in his voice. "Lay it on me, buttercup."

I opened my mouth, the words bubbled up in my throat, and—

Grinning, I hung up the phone.

Spock barked in approval.

My cell buzzed just before I pocketed it.

I'm gonna smack that ass.

I typed out my reply.

God, I hope so.

Then my phone was in my pocket and Pascal helpfully brought the crate inside the house. I locked up, looked down at Spock, and said, "I guess we should start our day, huh?"

Another little bark, followed by an earnest lick across my chin.

And hell if I didn't fall in love all over again.

TWENTY

AXEL

"I ought to smack *your* ass for pulling that shit with the alarm," she said two days later.

I leaned back on the bed, bending one arm and shoving it behind my head. "I'm down."

Her face froze for a second, surprise sliding through her expression, and I would have thought our video call had a bad connection if not for her shaking her head in the next heartbeat, mouth turning up at the edges.

"Christ, I want to fuck that mouth," I muttered.

Her mouth turned up further. "You've done that before."

"I want to do it again."

A shrug. "I'm down."

Groaning, I tossed my arm over my eyes. "Why must you torture me so?"

The audio went a little staticky, and I lifted my arm, stared through the phone and sweet Christ, why were we hours apart?

"God, I love your tits."

She grinned now, hands coming up, cupping her breasts, fingers drifting over her nipples.

"Squeeze them harder," I ordered, unable to stop myself.

"Bossy."

"Harder, honey."

Her hands tightened around the globes even as she gave me an order of her own. "Get naked."

I tossed back the blanket. "Already am."

Her laughter turned to a moan when I propped my cell on the nightstand, when I reached down and wrapped my fingers around my dick, stroking hard, knowing that I was pathetically close already. But then again everything about this woman did it for me.

Silky brown hair.

Curves for days. Wide eyes. Tan skin. Lips that begged for my cock to slip between them, begged for mine to be pressed to hers, tongue delving in.

And speaking of tongues delving...

Her pussy was a six-course Michelin-star meal.

And her ass...well, I'd discussed her ass already.

"Fingers between your thighs," I ordered. "Now."

"I'm not even naked yet." She did some phone-propping of her own, showed me that she was wearing a godawful pair of Care Bear pajama pants.

"Well, Christ, woman. Get naked."

"Why?" she asked innocently. "Is there some reason you might want me to take my clothes off?"

I had a hundred reasons.

A thousand.

But I couldn't verbalize any of them.

Instead, all I could manage was another command. "Open your nightstand drawer."

She stilled, hands on the waistband of those pajamas.

"Open the drawer."

A long, slow blink. And then she rolled, tugged open the

drawer, and I knew she saw it when her entire body went motionless.

"Naughty man."

"*Smart* man," I said. Then, "It's charged." A beat. "Put it in."

Her lips parted. Her eyes went molten.

And then she was naked.

And *then* she was putting it in, slipping the toy through folds I could see were dripping, the blunt tip disappearing inside her.

"That part goes over your clit," I rasped.

"I know how sex toys work," she said tartly.

"Do you?" I asked, hating to minimize the video of her, but having to as I opened the app. "Press the button on top."

She pressed it.

And her toy popped up on my phone.

Fuck yeah.

"What—?"

I'd thought about this a lot. I had a plan, though fuck if I could remember it. Instead, I pulled up the portion of the app that let me create my own rhythm. Create my own rhythm that would go to her phone, that would connect to the toy...and it would vibrate in the pattern I wanted.

The pattern I'd learned.

A pattern that had her gasping.

"What—?" she breathed.

I grinned.

And it was a fuck of a long way from my fingers stroking through her wet pussy.

But it was me, it was her, it was the best I could fucking do with the distance between us.

So I stroked the phone screen. I kept up with the pattern. I brought her to the brink...and then over it, my cock aching as she cried out my name.

It was bearable because it was my name on her tongue.

It was perfect because it was my name on her tongue.

It was—

She lifted her head. "Wrap your fingers around yourself."

"Buttercup. This wasn't—"

"And stroke hard until you come." She propped herself up on one elbow. "Pretend you're coming on me, on these—" She cupped her breasts again.

I could argue.

I could be chivalrous, make this only about her.

But...that wasn't me.

That wasn't her *and me.*

So I gripped my dick, stroked...and when I fell over the edge, my rough groan was only her name, over and over again.

———

I crossed my arms and waited, ass on the boards, feet on the bench.

"Too good for us, pretty boy?" Joel called as he skated by.

"Yup," I called back, but I was already hopping down, already moving toward him as he walked off the ice, his helmet pushed up, sweat dripping down his temples.

Bailey was at a planning meeting for the Winter Festival with Billie Rose.

I had the night off from hockey, though I'd need to leave early tomorrow to be back at the arena for a game—a game I was hoping that Bailey would join me at. So I was catching up with the guys and then, later, Bailey and I would meet up at Monroe's.

I couldn't wait to cuddle up with her at the bar, to steal sips of her beer and press my body to hers.

But, for now, I was watching the guys fuck around on the ice, wishing I could be out there.

My gear was in San Francisco.

Plus, it wouldn't do for me to get hurt practicing with a team that wasn't mine any longer.

I met up with Joel in the hall, and he was serious. For once.

"Your girl okay?" he asked, leaning against the wall and crossing one big skate over the other.

"Yeah," I said. "Thanks for looking after her until I could get her security sorted."

A nod. "That guy doing right by her?"

"Pascal is a professional."

"Fucker had scary eyes." He straightened slightly. "Though, just saying"—his mouth tipped up—"your girl has scary eyes, too."

"Asshole."

Joel grinned, pushed off the wall. "Of course, I think that mostly came from the fact that she was serious about wielding a shotgun."

"That she is."

Joel sobered. "That ex of hers is trouble."

"Yeah. We're working on tracking him down," I said. "Between him and Candi, I'm going to be paying Pascal for the next century."

Joel grunted and looked so serious that I gave him the rest.

"Pascal has a man with her at all times and installed an alarm system at her place. She's got a panic button to carry with her that goes straight to the police department and Pascal's office. Plus"—I smiled—"she's got her shotguns and clearly knows how to use them."

Joel held up his fist to bump. "Damn right she does."

I bumped it back. "Not sure that's something to celebrate when she's used them to threaten my balls more than once."

Joel smirked and lifted his fist again.

This time I didn't bump it.

But I did begrudgingly accept the punch on the shoulder.

"I'm gonna shower," Joel said. "And then we're going to light this town up!"

I punched him back. "In a very respectful, responsible way, correct?"

"Responsible?" Joel shrugged.

I shot him a look.

"Fine. Fine," he said both hands up in surrender. "But only because I don't want to hear it from Billie Rose if we start trouble again. Plus, we're finally out of the dog house and welcome at both bars in town again."

I grinned. "Progress."

"Respectful, though?" he asked, tapping a finger to his lips. "Don't you think that's asking a lot?"

"Fucker."

A smirk. "Damn right."

I rolled my eyes. "Ass."

"That too."

Sighing, I let my head drop back, stared up at the ceiling. "Why do I fucking bother?"

"Respectful," Joel said, surprising me. "Of the women and property only." A punch to my shoulder and fuck that hurt. Why the hell did Joel have to be so strong?

"As for you..." he added, clapping me on the side of the head and moving down the hall.

Jesus.

"*You,* however...I am gonna bust your balls at every *single* opportunity."

TWENTY-ONE

BAILEY

"And," Billie Rose said, typing on her laptop, "that is the last of my list."

"Thank fuck," Dessie muttered, grabbing her beer and finishing it off. "I've got to help Roger"—the owner of Monroe's—"behind the bar. Don't"—she pointed a finger at me—"let her sign me up for anything else."

I saluted.

Dessie grinned, started to say something back, but was cut off by the front door opening, boisterous laughter filling the air.

And my heart stopped.

"Aw." Dessie yanked at my ponytail. Not hard enough to truly hurt, but also not a light tug. "You're sooooo in loooove. Did you kiss his boo-boo from the other night, too? I know you were worried about *your man.*"

Sweet Christ. *This* was why I didn't have friends.

Heat at my back.

"She kissed me a *lot* of places," Axel said silkily, fingers trailing down my nape.

Billie Rose wrinkled her nose. "That's my niece you're talking about."

"That's my *woman* I'm talking about." I glanced up in time for him to stare down at me, to *wink* down at me. "And don't yank her hair," he told Dessie. "I like it on her head." He looked up at Billie Rose. "Especially since I like it dragging across my naked body."

There was a gagging sound and I turned to see that Joel had closed the distance between us.

"Give a guy a break," he muttered. "Not all of us are getting laid."

Billie Rose snorted. "Sure, Lothario."

Joel's eyes flashed. "What, harpy? I know it's been a few days for me, but how long has it been for you? So long that you only got dust up there?"

"Joel," Axel warned.

"I'll have you know—" Billie began, finger pointed in Joel's direction.

"Billie," *I* warned.

"Beer." Dessie plunked a pitcher on the table, having somehow made it to the bar and back while Billie Rose and Joel sparred. A stack of cups hit the table next. "Drink. And order some food so you don't get fucked up in my bar and start trouble."

"I resent that comment," Axel said lightly.

She tossed him a look. "The people of River's Bend have long memories."

Axel smirked. "Menus, bar wench." A clap of his hands. "Now."

Dessie poked him. "You're incorrigible, Axel Finnegan."

He grinned. "And I'm cute, too."

She grinned back. "Don't forget that you only got your boo-boo kisser because of me."

Billie Rose gasped. "Excuse me?"

Dessie plunked her hands on her hips. "I told him where to

find her *and* got him to take her home when she was sloshed after *two beers.*"

The look she shot me had me reaching for a glass, filling it.

Reminding me.

I was going to have my two beers, get pleasantly drunk, and then get pleasantly *fucked* by my man.

"I was the one who hand—" My aunt clamped her mouth together.

Axel shot Billie Rose a look. "Was the rest of that statement going to be —*cuffed?*"

"Why would you ask that?" Billie Rose asked innocently.

An innocence that no one near or at the table believed.

"I should thank you, I suppose," Axel said. "Because of those handcuffs—"

"And *I'm* done with this conversation." I slid out of my chair, my body brushing against Axel's as I shifted past him and moved into the booth, forcing Billie Rose to scoot in further. "My *man*" —I narrowed my eyes at Axel then at my aunt and Dessie in turn— "is here. Our dog is at home, probably trying to figure out how to escape his crate and destroy my new carpet. On the plus side, though, our work is done for the moment, and I've got a mind for some bar food."

Joel moved to the other side, along with a few other Rush players. I only knew one of their names since I'd met him on my porch —Ryan. Axel scooted in next to me, shoving me along the polished wood until I was pressed up against Billie.

And then he kept pushing.

Until Billie Rose and I were *both* sliding.

Until we were both sliding and the Rush players, including Ryan, abandoned the other side and were scooting into the booth behind Axel, filling in the circle-shaped booth.

And I didn't miss that somehow—and yes, that was me doing air quotes—in the shuffle, *somehow* Joel ended up next to Billie Rose.

I dropped my gaze to my hands, trying to bite back my smile.

"Jesus fucking Christ," Billie Rose muttered. "Just give me a second and I'll put my things away and—"

She was pushed up against Joel.

Who was busy glaring at Axel.

Billie Rose jerked.

"Cool it, harpy," Joel said, wrapping his fingers around her arm. A wicked smile on his face. "Unless you're going to crawl that sweet ass of yours into my lap."

Billie Rose's face went pink.

She glared at me. At Axel.

"Don't you dare touch me," she snapped.

"Just saying"—Joel's voice was golden silk, floating in the air— "*you* pressed yourself to *me*."

"Children," I warned.

My aunt glared.

But Joel seemed to relax, leaning back against the booth, throwing his arm over the top of it and manspreading...directly into Billie Rose's space. Then his eyes came to mine and there was none of the bravado. Not any longer. Only that gentle warmth he'd given me after I'd called Axel, that he'd given me after the call when he'd led me onto my porch, then into my living room, tucking a blanket around me and watching crappy TV with me as we waited for Axel to make the drive up.

A big softie under all that asshole.

Just like Axel.

What was it with these Rush men?

"I'm good," I told him. "Colt hasn't been back, and neither have my parents," I added when Billie Rose's gaze came to mine. "Axel's taking care of me."

My man pressed a kiss to the top of my head. "And she's fighting me every single step of the way."

"As one does."

It was a bit of a lie.

I was.

And...I wasn't.

It would be all too easy to fall into the trap of letting him take care of me.

Of forgetting myself and just *letting* him.

Become me. Telling me what I wanted, what I needed, *who* I was.

Which he understood. Because he just kissed me on the top of my head again, but didn't press any further, didn't tease me about that anymore.

"I went down to the planning department today," Billie said.

"What?" I asked, focusing fully on her.

She tucked her laptop into her messenger bag and then shoved the bag between her and Joel. "I think the developer Colt"—I smothered the chill that came through me at his name—"mentioned is Garret Smothers."

"Why does that name sound familiar?" Joel asked.

"Because he built that monstrosity of house you call yours," Billie Rose told him.

A shrug before he picked up the pitcher and poured himself a beer. "Real estate is a good investment."

"Not sure that real estate built on either side of a former fire-break is a smart investment, but I know he certainly made the houses *look* pretty."

Joel puffed up.

"What do you mean?" I asked before they could continue snapping at each other.

"Colt is his real estate agent."

I frowned.

"Colt has brokered properties for Garret all the way from Sacramento up to Tahoe. And Garret has wanted in on land in River's Bend for years."

"And Colt saw his way into River's Bend through me."

"Or through your parents," Billie Rose said. "They owned the property when you two were married, right?"

Yeah, they had owned it.

Until I'd bought them out with every last bit of savings I had, every bit of inheritance I'd received from Gramps and Gran, my retirement I'd cashed out early, money I'd borrowed from the bank based on paystubs for a job I quit to work the ranch.

My parents had cashed out their third.

Then they'd gone, to flit around, to ignore me, to live their lives for themselves.

As they'd always done.

I was an afterthought, *if* I was a thought at all.

"I would never sell the ranch," I whispered. "Not ever."

Axel went still next to me.

"I won't leave it. I won't. I *won't.*"

Billie squeezed my hand.

But Axel didn't react. He was a statue next to me.

I glanced up, stared deeply, but couldn't discern what message was in his bright blue eyes.

What was *hidden* behind those blue eyes.

Then he looked away and I lost them altogether.

His arm was around me; his thigh was pressed to mine. His scent was in my nose, his warmth surrounding me, his body was *right* next to me.

But he wasn't here.

And I had the distinct notion that I'd just lost Axel Finnegan.

TWENTY-TWO

AXEL

The arena was loud.

The ice was running fast.

But I was only focused on one fan in the stands.

Twelve rows back, just above the glass, though the netting that stretched from the top of the clear plexiglass to the rafters overhead would keep her safe from any stray pucks.

Because I was the type of man who thought about that now.

Worried about it.

Two weeks since that asshat had confronted her, and two weeks since she'd fired the shotgun that had left her with a scar on her shin.

And a glimpse of shadows in her eyes.

The memories gripping tight.

But between the alarm system and Pascal's man and Joel occasionally checking up on her and me going up whenever I could, she'd been safe, and slowly, the claws of her memories seemed to be easing.

The national anthem finished, and I rolled out my shoulders, got ready to focus on the game, on impressing my woman who was in the Gold Mine for the first time.

It was loud.

Then again, the fans had a lot to cheer about.

Three Cup wins since the team had been formed just over a decade and a half before.

A constant competitor in the playoffs.

They'd done everything right (after they'd begun very, very wrong).

So now they had camaraderie. No drama. No bad press. A fixture in the local community.

They were loved and successful and had die-hard fans.

All of that was why the Gold's home arena was known as one of the loudest stadiums in the league. And tonight the crowd was living up to that image. *Tonight,* they were cheering so loudly that it seemed to shake the rafters.

But the moment the puck dropped, the moment the game began, I didn't hear any of that.

I was a man possessed.

My woman was in the stands. My team was playing our rivals.

There would be big plays, big hits, and then, later, Bailey and I would fuck like rabbits and—

The player I was changing for sprinted to the bench, and I snapped into focus, jumping over the boards, landing on the ice and immediately springing into motion. The puck was heading toward our zone, the opposing team closing in on Brit, and I wasn't going to let Brit get scored on, not on my watch.

Certainly not with Bailey in the stands.

I sprinted into our zone, beelining straight for the player with the puck while Josh took the better angle and cut off the opportunity for the pass.

My breath hissed out as I shoved my shoulder into the other

player's, our bodies crashing together, our sticks clashing. We battled for the puck, and I earned stinging palms and a slash across the hands for my trouble, but I had the jump on him. I guided us into the boards, using strength and hips and ass and arms and shoulders and stick. And then as my breath hissed out again, the impact from the boards driving through my body, I used my feet.

To kick the puck over to Kayden.

He was moving with speed already, shooting toward me, and I held my breath as...he picked up the puck.

Yes!

Shoving off the fucker I'd been dealing with, I joined him in the rush, skating after him, accidentally—okay, on purpose—colliding with a Kings player who was jumping on the ice, getting in his way so that Kayden had a good chance at it.

He made excellent use of it as I pushed off my opponent, using the motion to slow me and shoot me forward.

Ha.

Fucker.

And then I was skating again, moving into the zone.

Kayden closed in on their goalie, shot, and...

Missed.

But I was there. And the puck was in the slot, and I could...*just* get my stick on it.

Not to shoot. Just enough to tap it to Rome who was streaking in.

Rome who buried it into the back of the net.

Hell *fucking* yeah!

I shot toward Rome at the same time Kayden did, the three of us crashing into the boards, rattling them, and while we were bumping fists, while we were exchanging "Fuck yeahs," my gaze drifted up. To Bailey.

Who was grinning like a loon and bouncing around in her Gold jersey.

I knew it had my name on the back.

Mine. *Mine.*

Damn, I was turning into a possessive fucker.

And I was living for every second of it.

She caught my gaze, waved, and winked.

And that felt...even better than assisting on this goal, even better than all the wins, all the success. It was better than *all* of it.

She was better than all of it.

Kayden punched my shoulder one more time, and I tore my gaze from Bailey's, from that wink and smile and all that mine, mine, *mine.*

I turned back, ready to focus on the game.

But as I did so, as I rotated around, spinning on the ice, ready to move to the bench, I caught a glimpse of blond.

Bleach blond.

Blinking, I started to turn back, to search the stands, the fans for that hair. It was distinctive. It was fake and bright and *blond.*

But then Kayden bumped into me as he started skating for the bench and I lost sight of it.

And when I glanced back, when I spared a moment to *look* even though I needed to get back to the bench so the game could keep moving, I didn't see any blond.

Just a sea of faces.

Dark hair, red hair, even some blue and green and purple hair. A variety of skin colors, light to dark and in between.

But no blond. Not a single strand of hair that light.

Not in the section in front of me, not in *Bailey's* section.

"Fuck," I whispered, still searching.

"Let's move it, boys," the ref yelled, and I knew he was talking to me, wanting me to get my ass into gear, knew that if I stayed long enough to search through every row, every section, every aisle to assure myself that the glimpse of blond wasn't Candi, and I risk a penalty for delay of game.

So, I forced myself to turn away, to skate to the bench.

But inside...fucking hell, *inside,* I was replaying that glimpse.

Replaying it over and over again.

Replaying it until I convinced myself that I hadn't seen it in the first place.

Twenty-Three

BAILEY

I showed my pass and they let me onto the elevator.

No lie, my hands were shaking.

I was about to go up to the family suite, to meet the rest of the team's wives and girlfriends and kids—or at least the ones at that night's game.

And it was because of the woman next to me.

Deep brown hair the color of dark chocolate, pale caramel eyes. A Gold T-shirt and simple black sweats.

And mischief written into each line of her face.

She'd come down to my seat during the final commercial break, introduced herself as Mandy, and invited me to meet her at the elevators after the game was over so I could "Meet everyone."

A fact that brought terror to my veins.

Mostly because she was...exuberant.

Even now the elevator car rose, she was practically vibrating next to me.

"You all right?"

"Uh-huh." She tossed a smile my way. "I just like getting in on the ground floor of these things."

"These things?"

"New relationships, making sure two people who are perfect for each other get their heads out of their asses so they can have their happy ending—"

"But Axel and I already love each other."

Mandy's face fell. "You do?"

"We do."

Such disappointment on her face, so much that I nearly laughed out loud. "Unfortunately, we've already figured out that we want to be together." A beat when she sighed and her shoulders slumped. "We've got other problems though."

A light in Mandy's eyes. "Problems?"

This time I *did* laugh.

"I have an asshole ex, freeloading parents. He has a woman obsessed with him and a selfish mother. We have four hours between us, and my career and responsibilities mean that I can't just move down here and his job keeps him best case, those four hours away, and worst case on the road for eight months out of the year."

It wasn't until I listed all of that out that I felt the weight of those obstacles, those problems.

"Let's start with the asshole ex."

My lips tipped up. "That's where Axel started, too."

Mandy's eyes warmed, but she didn't get to say anything because the elevator doors slid open and then we were stepping off the elevator and she was guiding me to the right, through a door, and...

Into chaos.

———

"And then you squish this together—"

My eyes went wide as I stared at the slime sliding through the little boy's fingers and dripping down onto his pants.

"Oh no," I said, reaching for the container and a pile of napkins.

"It's okay." He dropped his hand, scooping up the slime and leaving a trail of goo in its wake.

"Uh—"

A hand on my shoulder, one of the few men in the room. He had an adorable little girl propped on one hip and a gentle smile on his face.

He was also one of the prettiest men I'd seen in my entire life.

And I thought that, perhaps, all of that gorgeousness came from inside.

He was blissfully happy, and it showed.

"This one," he told me, snagging the napkins and making a good effort to clean up the slime, though there definitely were dredges left, bits that wouldn't come out. Not ever. "This one loves art, so his parents make sure to dress him in clothes that can get dirty." He smiled at me. "Especially on Art Night."

The door to the family suite opened and the little boy glanced up. "Daddy!" he yelled. "Look!"

And tore off straight for the tall, suited man striding into the room.

Who scooped him up and hugged him tight and there wasn't one—*one*—bit of hesitation for the slime in proximity to the clearly expensive suit.

No harsh rebukes.

No setting him away.

Just a hug between a father and a son and—

I turned away, my eyes burning, and quickly began consolidating the slime mess. I was jealous of a child...and sad for myself.

Very, very sad.

"I'm Stefan."

I glanced back up. "Bailey."

He grinned. "I know."

And then I processed his name, a name that even I—as a non-sports fan before dating Axel—knew. "Stefan?" I asked. "As in Stefan Barie?"

That smile widened. "I prefer Brit Plantain's husband."

The former captain of the Gold. The one who had turned the team from a league joke into a dynasty.

"Mama!"

My head jerked up, and then the toddler perched on Stefan's hip wriggled down, running across the room and clinging to her mother's legs.

"Nice to meet you," I said when it seemed like he was going to move away.

He squeezed my shoulder again. "It gets easier."

I blinked, brows dragging together.

His voice dropped. "That emptiness inside you. It shrinks and shrinks until one day..." A breath. "One day it's just gone altogether." His fingers tightened, and then he released my shoulder and moved across the room.

Slinging an arm around Brit's waist, kissing her cheek, ruffling their daughter's hair.

"It's her last season, you know."

I turned to see Mandy standing beside me again, her eyes looking misty. "I'm going to miss her."

"You've been friends for a long time?"

A nod. "Since the moment she first walked into this arena."

"That sounds wonderful," I whispered.

"She's the reason the team is like this"—a nod toward Brit, who'd picked up the boy covered in slime and blew a raspberry on his neck—"she's the reason we're a family."

"I—"

"She taught us—empty or full or in between. She taught us how to make a family. How to be loyal and how to tie us together so tightly we wouldn't break. Not ever." Mandy blew out a breath.

"It's a business. Of course it is. But it's also more. We're that family, that community, and you're part of that, too."

That sounded sappy as hell.

Too fucking sappy for my cynical heart.

I'd been a part of a family.

And their sole purpose, seemingly, had been to fuck me over time and time again.

But the part of me that loved Axel...that part of me wanted this to be true, wanted to be part of their big, happy family.

"You're not convinced," Mandy murmured.

"I—well—" I glanced up, saw Mandy's knowing gaze. "No offense, it's just..."

"Just what?" she asked when I trailed off and didn't finish.

"It's just—" A shake of my head. "That's not what I had growing up, and it's not like I'm really part of anything—"

"Bailey."

I opened my mouth, closed it.

"You'll—" She stopped. Then patted me on the arm as the door opened again and Axel walked in. My heart, oh God, my heart squeezed so hard that it felt like I would pass out.

I loved that man.

So *fucking* much.

And talk about sappy as hell.

"Give it time, honey," Mandy said, squeezing my arm again. "Just promise yourself that much, okay?"

My brows drew together. "I—"

Axel was getting close. I felt it in the tremor down my spine, the warmth in my belly.

Mandy nudged me forward.

"Go, honey," she whispered.

And then Axel's arms were around me, his lips were on my throat, and his mouth was at my ear, velvet rasp trailing along my skin. "Ready to go home, buttercup?"

TWENTY-FOUR

AXEL

"This is nice," she murmured, toeing off her shoes and leaving them on the rack by the front door before walking slowly through the kitchen. "Really nice."

"I know," I said, closing and locking the door, slipping behind her and wrapping my arms around her waist. "Probably the nicest place I've ever lived in."

I *had* to touch her.

I needed to touch her.

It was urge and calling and obsession.

She spun toward me. "Aside from my freshly remodeled house that you bankrolled, you mean?"

I smiled, tugging a strand of her hair, thankful all over again that Billie Rose had been willing to babysit both the ranch and Spock for a few days, despite the fact that the latter was proving to have a preference for his great aunt's heels. "Aside from that."

Fingers on my cheek, against my jaw. God, I loved it when she touched me like that. "Your place," I murmured. "Well, it feels like home. More than this apartment, as nice as it is. More than anywhere else I've ever spent time living in."

"Axel," she breathed.

"I mean that fancy carpet is like walking on a cloud."

She rolled her eyes, but she was smiling.

That was my favorite thing ever.

Her smiling.

"I mean it," he said.

Her smile gentled. "I know." A beat. "Which is why I'm gonna clean out a couple of drawers for you, clear some space in the closet." A kiss to my cheek. "You, sir, have just gotten the ticket out of Duffle Bag Life."

I chuckled.

"And tonight was..." She shook her head. "I've never been to a professional sports game. Not the Giants or Warriors or anything, and I've only seen you play on TV. And *God*." Her voice took on a breathless quality that had my cock twitching. "The crowd. The noise. The *speed*. You guys look fast, but until I actually was there, in the stands..."

Fucking beautiful.

She was fucking beautiful.

And she was talking about me.

Now that was the ego boost I probably didn't need, but the one I really liked anyway. "And what else?"

She swatted me. But she gave it to me anyway. "You were beautiful." A flash of white teeth. "And brutal. And *big*. You're *my* big, broody hockey player. But you're not even that big, not compared to some of the other guys."

I wrapped my fingers around her waist, drew her into the bedroom. "Ouch."

She blinked.

"Size matters, buttercup."

Another blink then she was giggling. "Does it really all come down to size then?"

"Of course it does."

She slipped her wrist free of my grip, turned and wrapped her arms around my middle. "You're big." Her lips turned up. "The *biggest.*"

Laughter bubbling in my chest. "Tell me more."

A tendril of heat in her eyes. "Really?"

"Tell me more about how watching your big, *big* man skate and check and *win* turns you on. Tell me more about what my big, hard body does to you, what it makes you feel. What it makes you *want.*"

She rose on tiptoe, and I bent automatically, so that her lips could reach my ear.

"It makes me want you all the time. Every second, every moment of the day."

I inhaled sharply when she nipped at my earlobe.

She dropped onto her heels, took my hand, and dragged it across her belly, fingers interlaced as she unbuttoned her jeans.

"It makes me go wet the moment I hear your voice, feel the heat of your body."

A shove and her jeans hit the hardwood floor.

"I've gone through so many pairs of underwear, drained the batteries of my vibrator more times than I could count, and—*here*—with you, fuck if it's a struggle not to melt into a puddle every moment you're near. Now"—she kissed my jaw—"have I stroked your ego enough?"

"My ego, yes. My cock, no."

Laughter in the air, something that was better than her giggles, her smiles. Something that roused the need, the possessive man inside me.

Claim. *Mine.*

Knock her over the head, drag her back to bed.

Her hand drew mine between her legs, to the scrap of fabric covering her pussy.

Soaked through.

She hadn't been lying.

Then again, she never did.

"Speaking of stroking," she murmured...spreading her thighs.

I might not be the brightest guy. I might not have gone to college, gotten a fancy degree. But I knew how to stroke a pussy.

With my fingers. With my tongue.

She gasped when I pushed her back, when I tumbled her onto the mattress, squatting at the edge and tugging her panties down her legs. But when she reached for the hem of her jersey, I stopped her. "Gonna fuck you in that, honey."

Pink on her cheeks.

Desire in her eyes.

Underwear...on the floor.

And I stroked.

With my fingers. With my tongue.

Tart and sweet. My woman on my taste buds. My name on her lips. I wanted to be inside her, wanted the tight heat of her surrounding me, clasping around me. But first, I wanted her to fall apart. On my fingers. On my tongue.

I sucked hard on her clit, and she gripped my hair.

I knew she was close, had been between her legs enough to read every movement, to know that she was going to come.

So, I spread some of her slick, wet heat down, back between the cleft of her ass, drifting over the tight rosebud, pressing lightly.

A gasp.

Her hips jerking against my face.

My name in the air.

I pressed harder, my finger slid in...

And she went crazy, bucking against me, pushing herself down onto my finger, clamping down on me front and back. I wanted my cock there. I *needed* it there.

But...

Not yet.

And then she was coming.

And then I was flipping her over, jerking her up onto her knees, sliding into her from behind.

She was still in the jersey, the hem of it rucking up and exposing that ass I was desperate to be inside. My name was emblazoned across her shoulders, and I was enough of a possessive male to fucking *love* seeing that.

My number.

My name.

Mine.

A flex of my hips and I was inside her tight wet heat, and fuck, *nothing* felt better than that. Than her.

Not being on the ice, playing in front of an arena full of fans. Not scoring a game-winning goal. Not even making her smile and laugh and giggle.

Though those were close.

But this...Bailey trusting me with her body, me bringing her pleasure...

The best fucking moments of my life.

I gripped her hips, ground deep.

"Axel," she groaned, back arching, pushing her body against mine, shoving herself against my cock, and loving every fucking second of it.

Fuck.

I was going to come.

I was going to come without her and—

She gasped.

I knew that hitch of her breath, knew that it meant she was close, that she was going to come, that I just needed to hold on a little longer.

Her pussy convulsed—

I lost it.

I thrust hard and fast and was barely aware that she was with me, that she was tumbling over the edge.

But I was aware enough, just that bare sliver of consciousness

—thank fuck, because *I* didn't come first, my woman came first— to keep going, to make sure her orgasm was long and sweet and completely finished before I collapsed, dragging us both to our sides on the bed, my lungs moving like bellows, sweat dripping down my back.

"I'm guessing"—she sucked in a breath—"you like the jersey?"

I groaned.

"What?"

I heaved myself up, flipped her over so she was facing me. "Now I have to fuck you again."

She smoothed her hand down my chest. "Another orgasm might kill me."

"But what a way to die." I waggled my brows. "I'm game to give it a try."

She giggled. "Another time." Then she yawned and cuddled closer. "Right now, I'm tired."

"Okay, buttercup."

I held her, stroking my hand through her hair, along her back, cupping her ass, letting my eyes drift closed, just for a moment.

Then I forced my body away from hers, went into the bathroom and cleaned up, coming back with a cloth, sorting her out despite her protests, and tucking her into bed. I got rid of the cloth, pulled on a pair of underwear, and crawled in next to her, loving the drowsy way she automatically curled into me.

As I held her close, I thought of how I'd planned to approach my offer, to explain about the modeling contracts and spokesperson offers, about Cole's charity, and Olivia's invitation for us to visit.

But I'd just had an orgasm that practically melted my brain.

So none of the explanations came out.

Instead, I just blurted, "Want to visit a different ranch with me?"

TWENTY-FIVE

BAILEY

This horse wasn't Data.

She was beautiful, with a deep chestnut coat and a sweet disposition.

But we didn't have the same mind meld that Data and I did, didn't have the same responsiveness, the same way of predicting what the other was going to do, almost before either of us did.

"What do you think?"

I turned and looked at the hockey player on the horse next to me, his blond hair gleaming in the sunshine.

He dwarfed his horse, was one of those players who made Axel seem small.

But he'd rode his mare like he'd been born in the saddle, and as a woman who'd spent a fair amount of time on horseback, I could appreciate the smooth, easy way that he moved.

"Your man gonna be jealous?"

I blinked, tore my gaze from Cole and his horse.

"Of me appreciating your horsemanship?"

A small grin. "Is that what you're appreciating?"

I eyed him up and down. "How is Axel the small hockey player?"

Cole's grin grew. "Sport's changing. Less about crushing people into the boards and more about skill and speed and finesse. That's why pretty boy"—he nodded to where Axel stood in the distance, a photographer next to him, snapping pictures of the camp's merchandise he was modeling—"is doing well. Decent sized, good foundations, great speed. Even *if* he's old for a rookie."

"And cheap for a model."

A shrug, his eyes dancing with mirth. "It's for the children."

Laughing, I kicked my horse, riding it up to the viewpoint Cole was taking me to while Axel's agent—and Cole's wife—Olivia, and Axel went about their business.

I was dating a model.

That was...hilarious.

But it was also amazing.

Because he was so much more than that. He made me happy. He was thoughtful and not the arrogant asshole I'd first thought he was. Yeah, he was a filthy puckboy, but I liked all those filthy things he did to me. How he touched me and treated me and—

I liked how he was with me.

"He's a good guy."

I blinked, realized I was daydreaming and missing the gorgeous view of the Pacific Ocean in front of me, beach visible in the distance, frothy white caps forming zigzagging lines over the tops of the waves as far as the eye could see.

Beautiful.

Prime real estate.

And Cole hadn't turned it into boring track houses, ruining the landscape all while making a hefty profit.

He was doing something good with it.

"I watched him." A beat. "You know. Watched him for years and wondered why in the fuck he was tanking his career." He paused, and I thought the answer, *knew* the answer.

His mother. What she'd done, supposedly in his name. *For* him.

Even though it was all for everything *she* wanted.

But I didn't speak it out loud.

Cole's expression was approving, and I turned back to the scene below, the scene we'd ridden from because Axel wasn't allowed to ride at the moment, not during the season. Wasn't allowed to do something physical like horseback riding that might result in an injury.

So he was back to being a pretty boy. I grinned, watched as Axel scooped up one of the kids he had been modeling with for the last couple of hours, plunked him on his shoulders and said something that made him laugh.

"He's a good man," Cole said softly.

"Yes, he is."

"I'm glad he's where he should be."

"Modeling for pennies on the dollar with that pretty boy face?"

Cole chuckled. "Damn right. Why do you think I married my shark of an agent?"

"She got you underwear modeling contracts?"

That was Axel's next job, posing in his skivvies.

More laughter. "No underwear. Not for me." A nod. "That one, though, I think he's game."

"Just because he's more comfortable naked than clothed?"

His lips twitched. "I may have heard about the handcuffs."

"My aunt is..." I shrugged. "Well, she has ideas and those ideas..."

"Sometimes result in handcuffs?"

Now I was chuckling. "You're terrible." A beat. "You're doing wonderful things at this ranch. But you're a terrible, terrible man."

His eyes still danced with humor. "Why does that please me?"

More laughter and then I watched Olivia turn toward where we'd paused, her gaze unerringly finding us. She waved.

Cole lifted his hand in answer.

"She can't ride in those heels?" I asked lightly.

A glance in my direction. "You'd be surprised."

I smiled. "You can go back," I murmured. "I'm gonna ride just a little longer."

Cole glanced at me. "If you keep going, the trail will loop and bring you back to camp in about an hour."

I nodded as he turned his horse around and disappeared down the trail.

————

It wasn't until I'd ridden for almost forty minutes before I realized that I'd been had.

The pergola was alight. There was a blanket on the ground, a couple of baskets, and a small outdoor heater.

And a hockey player.

Wearing a hoodie emblazoned with the ranch's name.

About an hour, my ass.

It'd be a hell of a lot longer than that after I showed Axel my gratitude for—

"Would it be a cliché out of one of your books if I helped you down so our bodies can brush together?"

"Yes." But I reached out to him anyway, shivering when his hands came to my waist and he lifted me off, slowly letting me slide along his body so that every inch of me brushed against every inch of him.

A perfect scene out of a historical romance book—minus the poofy dress.

But still yummy.

"Cliché," he murmured. "But a good one."

I arched against him, felt the length of his cock. "A *big* one."

His smile was a flash of white and then he was reaching behind me for the reins, tying them off on a hook before moving us to the gazebo.

"You don't need to woo me," I whispered.

"I do," he whispered back. "Forever and always."

I sucked in a breath. "You're not supposed to worm your way further into my heart, you know that, right?"

He kissed me.

And then I wasn't thinking about breathing, sucking in, letting it out, or anything in between.

"Plus," he said when we broke apart, casually, as though his chest wasn't heaving, same as mine. "I owe you a first date."

I grinned. "I think we're past that by now, don't you?"

He cupped my cheek. "Never." Then he drew me to the blanket, pulled me into the crux of his arms, long legs bent on either side of me. "Now. I know it only takes you two beers to get sloshed and start taking off your clothes, so"—he kissed the side of my neck, reached forward, and plucked out a bottle—"how many glasses of wine does it take to accomplish the same?"

I turned in the circle of his hold, watched as he poured for us, and smiled. "Let's find out, shall we?"

———

It had taken us much longer than an hour to get back to camp.

Mostly because we were lying on our backs under the gazebo, bellies full of wine and cheese and the homemade bread that I could have lived on for a long time.

For the next ten years at least.

For the rest of my life.

Now we were staring up at the night sky and I was pleasantly drunk and...

"What about the ranch?" he asked me. "When it's paid off. What will you do then?"

I sighed, watching Orion glimmer in the dark reaches of space.

"I'll go back to school. Live that dream of teaching annoying high schoolers."

His arm flexed behind my head. "You'd be a good teacher."

"I wouldn't make them read all that dry as hell 'classic' literature. I..." I smiled, remembering Mr. Lee, one of my favorite teachers at the many schools I attended over the years. "I'd be the cool teacher. The fun one."

"I know you would."

"Because I'm so fun?" I asked dryly. I'd done nothing but work for years, and that hadn't made me particularly happy or a joy to be around.

"You *are* fun." A kiss. "But I think you'd be good, mostly because you care."

That meant...*God*. That meant a lot. Even in my fuzzy, sloshy brain. "Honey," I began.

"I mean it, buttercup."

I knew that.

Which was why it meant so much.

"Honey—"

"I love you," he said. "You're obligated to accept my compliments."

"Axel—"

He bopped me on my nose. "Just accept the compliment."

Irritated—over accepting compliments (and yes, I understood exactly how asinine that was)—I pushed up on my elbow, rolled toward him. "I'm *trying* to take it. If you would just shut up and listen to me—"

He grinned, tweaked my nose. "I know, buttercup." Then his face went serious. "You know I'd pay for it, pay off the mortgage on the ranch, pay for you to go to school, pay for you to move down here or even pay for someone to manage the ranch if that's what you wanted."

And with that offer...

That was the moment I fell in love with Axel all over again.

TWENTY-SIX

AXEL

Her face went gentle in that way it often did for me.
That way I felt right in my heart.
The way that made me want to have her give it to me over and over again.

I lightly tweaked her nose and meant every word as I told her, "You know I'd pay for it, pay off the mortgage on the ranch, pay for you to go school, pay for you to move down here or even pay for someone to manage the ranch if that's what you wanted."

"Honey," she whispered after a long moment. "No."

"I—"

"*No.* Listen." She clambered on top of me, straddling my waist, and resting her hands on my chest. "This isn't something that you can convince me to accept. It isn't a compliment. It isn't you maneuvering around me so that I'll accept some repairs on my house." She stroked her fingers along my jaw. "This isn't something I'll *ever* accept. Gramps and Gran. They worked hard for that land. It's been in my family since the Great Depression, and I've done what I've done to keep it for us, for *them.*"

"I wouldn't expect anything back," I told her. "It would stay in your name, in your family's name."

"I know you wouldn't." A beat. "Because I know you. But it isn't for my sake or my grandparents' that I wouldn't accept that. I wouldn't accept it because of *you*."

That...stung.

"I—"

"*Listen*," she said again. "Your mother always needed something from you, always wanted it and demanded it, and I can't be like her—"

That whipped through me even more violently, even more sharply.

That *burned*.

"You're not her, not in the least." I gripped her arms, wanting to shake her because that notion was so *fucking wrong*. "Not *ever*. You couldn't ever be like her. Just—"

"Honey," she whispered. "Please. Just *listen*."

I wanted to continue denying it, to rebuke every single bit of bullshit that was currently sliding out of her mouth, to reproach it for the vitriol it was.

But...she'd asked me to listen.

So, I shut up and did so.

"Sweetheart," she said, more gently than she had ever spoken to me. I loved the sass, loved when she snarked back at me, when she was fire and spine and steel. But the soft, the gentle, the way it was just for me, *only* for me...

That burned in a way that was all that much more acutely painful.

That stole my breath and made it hard for me to focus on her words rather than kissing her, *fucking* her under these stars until both of us sank into oblivion.

"You can't pay for my school, my home, my life. You can't because not only do I need to understand that I can take care of myself, but you need to as well. You need to know that I'm okay on my own."

"God, Bailey," I said, sliding my hand up and cupping her cheek. "You're the most capable person I know."

"You need to know," she said again, "that *I'm okay on my own.*"

I inhaled. "Bailey."

"I'm in this. I love you. Not for what you can give me," she whispered, "but because I would be okay on my own without you, without your help, and despite the fact that I *don't* need you, I *choose* to be with you."

I inhaled sharply.

Deeply.

That struck...deep.

"Buttercup."

"I choose *you*. Not some sexy, up-and-coming hockey player who's a pain in my ass."

"I—" A shake of my head. "What?"

"I choose *you*. Not a meal ticket or a man who can do something for me. But you. *Axel Finnegan.* The man I love. The man who loves me back." She wrapped her fingers around my wrist, held my palm to her cheek. "Not for *any* other reason aside from the fact that you own my heart."

My eyes stung. "Fuck, Bailey."

"Do you understand?"

I understood, every *inch* of me understood. I nodded. "I understand."

"So, you'll promise—no maneuvering around me and doing things like going to my bank and paying the mortgage behind my back?"

I scowled.

"Finnegan," she warned. "Promise me you'll let me handle that on my own."

I didn't want to. But I understood, what she needed. What *I* needed. I blew out a frustrated breath. "I promise."

She softened. "Thank you."

"Anything," I whispered. "Anything for you."

Laughter...turning wicked, taking the seriousness out of the moment as she asked, "Anything?"

I slid my hand into her hair, doubled down. "Anything."

"Good," she murmured. "Because I want to teach you to ride."

Frowning, I started to sit up, but she pressed me back down. "You know I can't—"

A nip to my jaw, my throat. "I want to teach you to ride *me.*"

Now *wicked* turned my laughter rich and husky. "That"—I flipped us—"I don't need any lessons in."

A raised brow. "Oh?"

I reached for the button of her jeans, smirked. "Oh yeah, buttercup."

———

"Do you ever think you would move?" I asked.

Her eyes shot to mine, a glimmer of hurt in the chocolate depths.

"I'm not saying to get rid of the ranch," I said quickly, knowing how that came off after all we'd just talked about. "I get how important it is to you." I tugged her closer, held her tighter. "I just...when you manage to pay off the debt, are able to hire someone to manage everything...would you live somewhere else?"

She paused.

For a long time.

Then, "I don't know."

That stung, hurt deeply, even though it shouldn't have. We loved each other, yes. We were together. I wanted her forever.

But we were new.

She wasn't just going to uproot her life, not after she'd fought so hard to cling tightly to it.

I just...kind of wanted her answer to be like, *"Yeah. I want to*

*live with you. Wherever that might take you. Even if you're traded.
Even if you move halfway around the world, I'll be with you."*

"Would you?" she asked.

"I'm used to living wherever," I said. "I don't care where I end
up. So long as that's with the people—the *person*—I love."

She inhaled. "Speaking of that."

Now *I* inhaled. "Yeah?"

"I was kind of hoping that you would stay."

I frowned.

I mean...I did stay. Every time I was up in River's Bend, I
stayed at her place.

"You know, 'cause the long-distance stuff sucks," she said. "So,
I was thinking that like...maybe in the off-season you could stay,
you know, with me, and then make the ranch your home during
the rest of the time—when the hockey schedule allows it...to—
and I—"

Funnily enough, her nervousness relaxed me.

It meant she cared enough about me, about us, to be nervous.

And that allowed me to find my way back to me. My annoying,
cocky alter ego. The one that she pretended to hate, that she loved
despite the fact that it exasperated her, the one that brought out
her sass and fire.

Which *I* loved.

"You asking me to move in with you, sugar?"

"I—that's what I—" She froze, her face a mask of disgust.
"*Sugar?*"

I grinned, nipped the tip of her nose. "Yeah. Goes well with
buttercup, don't you think?"

"Uh, no—"

"No? Okay, well then, it goes well with *honey.*" *I waggled my
brows.* "*Or syrup?*"

A groan, though her eyes flashed with heat, hopefully at the
memory of my culinary delights. "You're the worst, Axel
Finnegan."

"And by the worst, you mean the best?"

I felt the look she shot me in my cock, as though her fingers had wrapped around it. No. Her mouth, her tongue. "The. Worst."

I shifted closer, trailed my fingers down her spine. "Can I negotiate for more dresser space?"

She swatted me, but now her lips were curving. "Seriously. The. *Worst.*"

A kiss to her jaw. "Hanging room in the closet?"

"The—"

I flipped her over, pinning her between my legs, cupping the side of the throat. "You gave me two drawers, buttercup."

Teeth pressing into her bottom lip. "Yeah."

"You gave me your heart," I said simply.

A roll of her eyes. "I told you I loved you. It's not like I served the organ up on a platter."

"You gave me *you.*"

Her body softened. "I...well...yeah," she whispered.

"Then, as long as I'm with you, I'm home."

That had her lips parting, her eyes warming.

"Yeah," she agreed.

"And have two drawers."

Bailey let her head flop back onto the ground with a groan. "The. Freaking. *Worst.*"

But then she kissed me.

And if that was the *freaking worst,* then I would happily take it every day for the rest of my life.

Especially when she straightened, smirked down at me, and said...

"Okay, I'll give you a third."

Twenty-Seven

Bailey

I'd spent three days with Axel.

In. A. Row.

It was the most since he'd gotten the call-up.

And it had been filled with bickering and fucking and watching him play and lying out beneath the stars...and more fucking and more bickering.

And it had been the best three days ever.

Now, I had to say goodbye and go back to my lonely life without my boyfriend's big cock, and—

Boohoo.

Poor me.

Grinning, I turned off the highway and began weaving through town, eager to get home and see my pooch and my horse and my steer, even as I was mentally crafting the saucy text I was going to send.

Maybe something about how he was going to have to *earn* his three drawers.

Perfect.

That would be perfect.

Couldn't make it *too* easy on him. When we sparred verbally—or otherwise—and he got all growly and turned on...

Chef's kiss.

That would be perfection.

And then I would have a week's worth of saucy to send his way, a week's worth of pent-up Axel Finnegan...and how so sad I would be to have to deal with the fallout from that pent-up week apart, from the mood he'd be in when he came up next Tuesday.

Oh, the humanity.

My cheeks were hurting because I was smiling so widely, but I didn't even care how much of a dork I was.

I was happy.

I was dating a sexy model hockey player with a big dick and a bigger heart.

I was *happy*.

I'd spent too much of my life being miserable to worry about being a dork when I was finally happy.

In fact, I hit the button to roll down my window.

Stuck my head out, felt the wind on my face. "I'm happy!" I yelled into the air. "I'm happy!!"

A dork.

But a happy one.

At least until I turned into my driveway and saw...

It.

———

There was a real estate sign on my driveway.

Right there, staked into the ground.

Like it belonged there.

Like I'd asked for it.

Like I *wanted* it.

For Sale.

Smothers Holdings.

I'd parked. I'd stopped and parked, staring at the abomination in my driveway, knowing instantly it was Colt, that he'd done this.

That he'd think I would just roll over and die and *accept* this.

That *motherfucker.*

I got back in Gramps's truck, mentally pulling in further, parking next to the barn, like I did every time I came home.

But then...

Something came over me.

Maybe something as cliché as a cold rage. Maybe something simpler, hotter, burning through me. Maybe something—

My foot hit the gas.

The sign made a satisfying *crunch* as it succumbed to the heavy iron rust bucket that was Gramps's truck.

I reversed.

Heard that crunch again.

And I smiled.

———

I was still smiling when I pulled up to the offices of Smothers Holdings, Spock in the passenger's seat, happy for the ride. Admittedly, I was less happy and my smile had become more of a grimace in the hour-plus drive to Sacramento.

But my lips were parted. My teeth were showing.

I was smiling.

I was holding on to my happy.

By pure dint.

Screeching into a stall, I shoved out of Gramps's truck. "Stay, Spock," I ordered, cracking the window for him, thankful it wasn't hot. I slammed the door and reached into the bed of my truck, grabbing the largest remaining chunk of the real estate sign. Then I was in through the sliding glass doors.

A receptionist at the half-moon-shaped desk glanced up at me. "Can I..."

"Colt. Where is he?"

"I—I'm sorry. Mr.—"

"Where is he?" I asked on a hiss.

"I—"

Fuck it.

I moved past the desk to the directory posted on the wall. It didn't take long to find him. Not too many assholes named Colt in this world.

And then I was striding down the hall, carrying the sign behind me, barreling toward his office...

Only to find it empty.

That was...disappointing. Infuriating.

Laughter.

Not mine. I hadn't completely lost my mind—not yet, anyway. It was...*his.*

Spinning in a circle, I saw the receptionist had come my way, but I wasn't going to get bogged down in her bullshit, so I moved further, walking away from her.

Spotting him.

Through the window of a conference room.

Perfect.

I shoved through the door, enjoying the shock on the three men's faces when the strange woman with a broken sign burst in—strange to all but one of them, anyway.

I dropped that sign on the wide conference table, smirking when they jumped.

"Baby," Colt began.

It settled frost between my shoulder blades.

"Who're they?" I asked.

Colt's eyes narrowed, taking on a dangerous glint.

"I'm Garret Smothers," the taller of the three said. I should have figured, just based on the expensive suit alone.

I turned to the other man. "And you?"

"*Bailey.*"

A snapped-out rebuke.

One that used to have me rocketing to attention, have me cowering and treading carefully so that he wouldn't lose it, wouldn't step over that edge.

Careful. Careful.

Don't crush any of those shells.

"John Wilkens."

"Owner"—I nodded at Garret—"lackey"—to Colt—"and...?"

"Co-owner," John said.

"Ah."

A pause, long and drawn out. Then Garret spoke. "And you are?"

"His ex-wife."

The pause was longer this time, more drawn out.

"Want to know why we divorced?"

"Bailey—"

"He beat the shit out of me." Taut air, Colt jerking, taking a step toward me. But I held my ground. "Not once," I pressed on. "*Many* times. But the worst time, the final straw for me was when he broke my ribs and gave me a concussion, when he hit me so hard, so many times that I thought I was going to die in our house." A breath. "So, I ran out, barefoot, not giving a damn that it was raining, that my feet were sliced to shit by the time I got safely away. All I wanted was to get away from *him.*"

"A typical ex-wife," Colt sneered. "Spewing vitriol and—"

"Lies?"

It brought me great satisfaction to cut him off.

"I have pictures," I said softly. "Billie Rose made me take them, even though I wouldn't press charges back then. She made sure I had proof." I turned to John and Garret. "Would you like to see them? Like to see what your employee did to me?"

Colt lurched toward me, fist raised. "You—"

But I wasn't afraid. "There it is." I nodded at his fist, at his expression. "There's the man who hurt me. But," I said, glancing over at John, at Garret, "you probably don't give a shit about him, about me. I do think that you give a fuck about a man illegally listing properties."

Two pairs of brows rose.

"Your parents—"

"Don't own Russet Ranch," I snapped at Colt. "*My* name is on the title. *I* am the one who pays the mortgage. *I* am the one who will decide to sell"—I leaned forward—"and *newsflash*, asshole. I will never agree to sell my home. *Never.*"

I turned back to Garret. "Now I know you've had run-ins with Billie Rose. I know what it's like to have her not be happy with you, the trouble she can bring for you." I narrowed my eyes. "I'd advise you to stop fucking with me, with my land, with the people of River's Bend."

"Now, little girl, I'm not much for hurting women." Garret's gaze pinned me in place. "But I don't take to threats kindly."

"It's not a threat."

I pointed at the sign.

"That is a sign of you overstepping. That is a sign of *him*"—I pointed at Colt—"overstepping in River's Bend. That is the truth. That is *fact*. And if you *really* want to build, want to be part of the future of our town, then don't pressure people. Don't push. Wait for them to sell and then buy your land, build your houses."

Garret rocked back.

"That's not a threat. That's free...*advice*."

I thought I saw a smile on Garret's face, but then Colt was grabbing my arm, jerking me to face him, and—

Suddenly he was six feet away from me, pinned to the wall, and...

Pascal had an arm pressed to his throat.

"You will *not* touch her."

"I—"

Pascal pressed harder, hissing, "You will *not* touch her because if you do, I will *destroy* your life. And *that's* a threat. And *that's* advice—advice I really hope you won't follow because, fuck, what I would *give* to have the opportunity to destroy you piece by piece by *piece*. Now," he said even more intensely, "if you think that I'm going to leave her open for you to take some kind of fucked up revenge, to come back and hurt her as punishment, then think again. I will be *watching*. I will be *waiting* for you to come, to make a mistake, and I will love fucking tearing you apart."

The silence that stretched was quiet, was long, was almost smothering.

And all the while, Colt was turning purple.

I supposed I should be frightened of Pascal, of how he could move, of what he could do. He was effortlessly subduing the man who'd beaten me half to death and not struggling in the least.

He could...he could wreck me.

I just knew that he wouldn't.

Garret broke the silence. "I'll make sure the listing for your property is removed."

"Thank you."

More silence.

Then, "Now, if you don't mind, we have a meeting to finish."

I glanced from Pascal and Colt to Garret and John...

And suddenly I was tired.

So, I just nodded, left the sign where it was, and went out to Gramps's truck.

Not surprised when Pascal met me there, gentle hand on my shoulder, eyes searching my face.

A smile curved his mouth.

"You're going to be okay, Bailey Donovan," he murmured.

I looked at the splinters in the bed of my truck, looked inside *myself*, and I knew he was right.

"Yeah," I whispered.

"Go," he ordered softly. "It's getting late."

"Okay. And...thanks—"

"No thanks necessary."

"I know." I covered his hand with my own. "But thank you all the same."

His face gentled. "We'll keep an eye on you, just to make sure he doesn't decide to do something about that bruised ego."

"Now you're just asking for more gratitude."

A soft groan. "I'm going now."

"Pascal?"

He turned back. "Yeah?"

"Thank you. I mean it. For everything."

"Always." A beat, his lips turning up at the edges. "And remind me to never get on your wrong side."

"Just saying, that's down the barrel of my shotgun."

A grin. "Noted."

And then...

He was gone.

Melting into the shadows. Disappearing from sight.

Gone.

But I knew he was still watching over me as Spock and I drove home.

Twenty-Eight

Axel

It wasn't until a week later that I got the full story of what had happened between Colt and Bailey.

Bailey had given me a bit.

Pascal filled in some more.

But it hadn't been *all* of it.

Not until Bailey had laid it out to me that night, lying on the couch, Spock curled up beside us as we watched a stupid movie on TV, belly full of beer and junk food.

Properly plying me so that I'd take it okay.

No surprise, I didn't.

I hadn't.

How could I?

She'd driven right to her ex, to the ex who had hurt her.

Pascal said she'd been amazing.

Bailey said *he'd* been amazing.

And I...I hadn't been there.

Rage had boiled through me, along with guilt, with disappointment. I *hadn't* been there.

"This is some of that *you have to see that I can take care of myself* bullshit, isn't it?" I'd grumbled.

Which had her cracking up.

Which had her body moving against mine in all the right ways.

Which had led to me moving against her in the *all* the right ways.

Now, she was in the bath and I was unpacking my stuff...into three drawers, thank me very much. But as I went through my duffle, shoving sweats and extra underwear into my drawer, my fingers caught on a folder.

Frowning, I pulled it out, flipped through the pages.

And realized what an idiot I was.

Weeks ago, I'd had someone write up a valuation for the ranch, wanting to know what it was worth, how much was left on the mortgage. How I could help Bailey dig out of her hole.

But then I'd made that annoying—albeit both logical and touching—promise.

To let her make her own way.

And this was worthless.

I'd still thought to show her, just so she knew, had all the information, but after Colt and the For Sale sign and that drive down to Sacramento...

Well, it could all wait.

I shoved the papers in the back of the drawer.

Later I'd show her and she could marvel at how much the land had increased in value, how much equity she now had.

Today, tonight, right *now*, she needed the issue of anything happening to the ranch that didn't involve horses, fencing, cows, and hay to be shoved away, to be forgotten.

I shoved in my final pair of jeans and shut the drawer.

Then I turned for the bathroom and smiled.

She was taking a bath.

I'd see if she wanted a companion.

And then I wouldn't take no for an answer.

———

Lucky for me, I found that Bailey was always up for a bath buddy.

———

"You know you've just bought yourself hot cocoa duty at the Winter Festival," Billie Rose said, sitting down next to me and sipping deeply from the mug of hot chocolate I'd made her.

"I think I'm busy that night."

Billie glanced over at me, blond curls bobbing.

"You're not."

Unfortunately, she probably knew my schedule better than I knew it.

So I didn't argue.

"It feels weird to be on this porch with you and not be naked or handcuffed."

She just sipped innocently, eyes in the distance where Bailey had disappeared, riding Data, Spock at their side. "For the record, you were too drunk to remember being naked or handcuffed with me on this porch."

I chuckled. "You know, I never did ask you why you did that."

"Didn't you?"

I just shot her a glare.

"You already know that you like to get naked when you get drunk"—she slanted a look my way—"something you and Bailey have in common."

My glare didn't shift. "And the handcuffs?"

"I had to make sure you didn't wander off." A shrug. "There are dangerous creatures around—rattlesnakes, mountain lions. Hell, we even get the occasional black bear that has wandered out of Tahoe and down through the basin. I wanted you for Bailey, not to be out meandering naked and getting yourself killed."

Woman had a point.

"Did you consider that it was closer and easier to take me to my apartment?"

She took another sip from the mug. "I consider everything."

"Including Joel?"

The mug hit the step next to me with a soft *clink*.

"Joel is an ass."

I nodded. "He sure is. Though he's a *good* ass."

"Is there such a thing as a *good ass?*"

"Yes," I said simply.

She rolled her eyes, picked up her mug. "And anyway, Joel has no bearing on anything. I'm just glad that he's stopped tearing his way through my town." A beat. "Though, you have something to do with that."

I lifted my brows at her. "Though, I could say that *you* had more to do with that."

Billie didn't reply to that, just sipped her hot cocoa and sat silently next to me.

"I never did thank you." A breath, and I forced my tone to be light. "For the handcuffing and the nakedness. *Both* times."

"You're welcome for the handcuffing." She sipped again. "Though not for the nakedness, as we've established that was all you."

"One of my many talents."

"I'm not joking about the hot cocoa for the Winter Festival, you know."

I reclined against the porch pillar. "I know. I'll send you the recipe so that you can have the proper supplies on hand."

She drained her glass, placed it next to her. "If you need extra practice, I'm here as an official taste tester."

"Taking one for the team?"

"Taking one for my hips." She tapped the top of her cup. "And speaking of which...please, sir, my hips would like another."

I laughed, picked up her mug, and stood. "Only one refill per customer. Both for you." A beat. "*And* your hips." A flash of white teeth, her chuckle filling the air. "Plus, Bailey would have us both on the wrong end of her shotgun if we didn't save her any."

"True." I moved to the door. "Though, just saying, Axel..."

I paused, glanced back.

"If you make another batch..."

I lifted my brows.

"It'll give you more practice for the Winter Festival *and* make sure we have enough for Bailey to have seconds"—her smile widened—"or *thirds*, if the batch happens to be big enough."

Sighing, I shook my head.

"Good thing Bailey now has a really big pot."

"And lots of chocolate?" Billie asked hopefully.

"And enough chocolate to fill that really big pot."

Billie Rose grinned.

And I followed the unspoken command.

More hot chocolate, hockey wench, I imagined her order.

So, I was smiling as I moved back into the kitchen and made more hot cocoa.

More for me. For Bailey. And one more for Billie Rose.

And her hips.

TWENTY-NINE

I was an elf.

Not a sexy elf.

No short green skirt, striped green and white tights.

Just pointed ears, a jaunty hat, and a whole lot of ugly moss and scarlet-colored sweater. With embroidery.

And my man was looking like a snack in a simple polo under a tight black jacket with the Gold logo emblazoned over his heart.

Color me surprised that he had a hot chocolate recipe at all.

And extra surprised that it was fucking delicious.

So delicious that his line was longer than mine.

Though that was probably because he was there and Joel and Ryan had been signed up to help, so there was a trio of hockey yumminess offering cheap chocolate goodness to the masses.

Instead of an unsexy elf with stale candy canes.

Okay, fine.

They probably weren't stale. Billie Rose wouldn't let that happen.

But a woman had to have her excuses.

"I want to see Santa!"

I turned away from my yummy neighbors and glanced down at the little girl. Now *she* looked like a cute elf, complete with the proper outfit—red shoes, green sweater dress, those striped tights I really was going to have to buy for next year.

"Come on," I told her. "You can go right to the front of the line."

Tiny brows pulling together. "There is no line."

Small details.

And too smart for my good.

I unhooked the velvet rope (see? Billie Rose was on point about those details) and ushered her toward the big, red-suited man.

"Make sure you have your list ready!"

The little girl ran forward.

I manned the camera, got the obligatory pictures, and set about printing them out, trying to pretend that I hadn't noticed Billie Rose glaring at Joel from the homemade snow station. We didn't get snow where we were, other than the odd twenty-year storm with an inch or two of snow that didn't really stick. Hail was more likely, though it still didn't stay long on the ground or come all that frequently.

In the distance, there was a small ice rink, and I could see that some of the other Rush players had been roped in to give lessons.

There were lots of happy kids swarming around their legs.

And lots of happy women gathering close, staking their claims, trying to get their hot hockey man for a night or a month or a lifetime.

I was one of those women now, I thought with a small smirk.

Hooked my star to my hot hockey guy.

Grinning, I printed the picture of my cute elf girl and Santa then stuck it in one of the precut cardboard holders that had been ordered for this event. Some foam stickers, a candy cane (not stale) joined it in the bag that I passed over once she'd finished talking to Santa.

By then, my stall was seeing some action, and the next hour of my life was a flurry of ushering kids forward, printing pictures, passing out stickers and candy canes and the occasional hug.

My feet hurt.

My *newly* pointed ears hurt.

My brain hurt.

A hand on my nape, lips at the base of that pointed ear, a warm body shuffling me off to a shadowed alley. "The line—"

"You're on break."

I glanced back, saw that I indeed had been relieved by Dessie, who winked at me and waved me off.

A nudge forward, sending us further away from the bustle of the festival, tucking us into a shadowed alcove, his front to my back, his arms around me. His tongue flicked out, traced the shell of my ear beneath the prosthetic. "These are hot."

I shivered.

"And I'm gonna fuck you in them tonight."

I bit back a moan, started to straighten, but his hands came to my hips, holding me in place.

"That sweater is ugly as sin though." A nip to my earlobe. "I'm going to get that off you and burn it."

"It is *not* ugly."

That was a lie.

My sweater was ugly as sin.

He bent so that his chin rested on my shoulder. "Are these supposed to be candy canes?"

Palms sliding up my sides, stopping just beneath my breasts.

I tilted my head back, nipped at his jaw. "My candy canes aren't ugly."

"Hmm." His fingers drifted, slightly brushing the underside of my breasts, where the curve of the candy canes dipped down. "This sweater is."

I pinched the back of his hand. "Enough about the sweater."

"I'm only stating the truth."

I spun in the circle of his arms, glared at him. "See if I show you *my* candy canes later."

"Just saying, I've spent a lot of time between your thighs, and I haven't seen evidence of any candy canes." A kiss to the tip of my nose. "Though maybe I should buy you some red and white striped lingerie, make you my own personal candy cane, and lick every inch of you."

That was so cheesy.

But fuck if it didn't send a shiver through me.

Sigh.

This man had me so wrapped around his pinky finger it was pathetic.

"If I *had* a candy cane," I said begrudgingly. "I wouldn't let you see it now that you called my sweater ugly."

A nip to the side of my throat. "I bet I could convince you to show me."

"I—"

"What?" He flicked his tongue out. "You think I'm lying?"

He could probably convince me to do anything.

But I couldn't admit that.

"I think that you don't *think* you're lying," I prevaricated.

"Oh now, buttercup." Teeth on my throat, my jaw. "Them's fightin' words."

His hand dipped down, the roughened fingertips brushing against my skin. Oh yeah. I liked the fighting words, liked what they brought me.

How they felt drifting against my clit.

"How are you going to fight me?" I asked breathlessly.

He stepped forward, pressing me against the wall, hand sliding lower, dipping through my wetness.

Yup.

I was wet.

Sigh.

"Hold this for me."

The cup was plunked in my hand and my heart squeezed hard at that glimpse of his huge soft center beneath all my big broody hockey player. Taking care of me.

Bringing me hot cocoa.

Loving me.

I grabbed onto the cup and then his hand was smoothing back along my belly, this one drifting up instead of down, dipping beneath my bra, massaging my breast, dragging across my nipple.

I bit back a moan—

"Bailey."

I stiffened, but didn't get a chance to move before his hands were out from beneath my clothes and I was tucked securely behind him, his big body in front of me, between me...

And I peeked my head around.

Fucking hell.

Axel stood between me and...my mother.

THIRTY

AXEL

What. The. Fuck?

I was trying to get my girl off into the shadows, to sneak a kiss, a touch, a—

Okay, a quick orgasm for her. A chance to cop a feel for me.

But now her mother—*her mother*—was standing there and—

Seriously.

"What. The. Fuck?" I muttered. "Go away."

"I need to see my *baby!*"

Now her voice was rising, and it was shrill. That awful type of screech that had my eardrums aching in protest.

"I want to see my baby. I need to see her and—"

She *was* shrill.

So I went for calm, strived for calm, held it by the tips of my fingers. Barely.

"This is not the way. If Bailey wants to talk to you, she'll reach out."

Tears in eyes that looked like Bailey's, in a face that looked like the woman I loved...except wrong. "*If* she wants to see me? If my own daughter wants to see me?" A tear slid down her cheek. "My *own* daughter!"

Sweet Christ.

She was exhausting and manipulative and I knew that it was pure show, not only because of what Bailey had told me about her.

But because she reminded me of my own mother.

Which, admittedly, wasn't the best place for my mind to go. Not when I wanted to be calm and in control and steady for Bailey.

"You need to go," I gritted out.

"I will not—"

"Just to clarify, I *know* she doesn't want to see you." I gestured down the street. "So, fuck right off out of her life."

Just that quick, the tears and shrill were gone.

"How do you *know?*" she snapped. "She hasn't sent me away now, has she?"

"I want you to go," Bailey said, calm and steady and...*all Bailey.*

Bailey's mother sputtered. "Wh-what?"

"How could you possibly think that I would want you in my life?" she asked. "After *everything.* After my childhood and the chaos, the selfishness of you and Dad." She paused. "Who's where, by the way?"

"What?"

"Where's Dad?" Bailey asked.

Her mother stiffened.

"Yeah," Bailey said softly. "He's not here. He's *never* around—not when I needed him, probably not when you needed him, either. He might as well be a traffic cone, standing useless and off to the side."

Eyes flashing, Bailey's mother sucked in a breath. "Your father isn't the point. I sacrificed everything for you and—"

Bailey chuckled.

"My life was about—"

"You," Bailey finished. "It was about *you*." A breath. "Because you've never given me something without strings. Not once."

"I carried you in my *belly*—"

"I'll amend my statement. You've never done anything for me beyond keeping me alive." Bailey stepped up to my side, wrapped her arm around my waist, and leaned close. "And that's more than some people get, so, lucky me, right?"

"I—"

She cut her mother off. "But I wasn't lucky. I was stuck with you, with Dad, with that chaos and drama and sneaking off in the middle of the night, moving before someone could come after us for overdue rent, always being forced to leave things behind, never able to trust that the connections I was making were going to be for a few days or weeks or months, if the time was going to be so short that it was pointless to get attached—"

Her voice broke and I laced our fingers together, held tight to her hand.

I wanted to step in.

Wanted to sweep her away.

But...she needed to do this, needed to do it for herself...

And...

She needed to do it for me as well.

Because seeing her like this, understanding this part of her— the strength in the face of pain, the courage to keep pushing—and the pride I felt for her...

Well, for a moment, it even eclipsed the love I had for her.

Just for a few seconds.

Because then the love was swelling up, sucked back like water along the ocean floor, resembling a beach before a tsunami and then the wave was slamming forward, crashing into me, eclipsing every emotion in me.

Except love.

Then it was just *love*.

"You did that," Bailey whispered. "You hurt me over and over again. But I could have forgiven you then if not for how you acted when I came to you about Colt." Her voice raised. "You encouraged me to go back to him. After he beat me. *Me.* Your daughter." She shook her head. "*That* was the moment I knew that you wouldn't love me or maybe *can't* love me, maybe you can't love anyone but yourself. Because if you did, if you actually cared about me...how could you send me back?"

I squeezed her hand, trying to temper my fury, mindful of my strength, not wanting to hurt her, not ever.

Because she'd been hurt too much already.

"You did all of that and then you *still* went behind my back and tried to sell the ranch. The *ranch!* Dad grew up there." She tossed up her free hand. "For all intents and purposes, I grew up there, too. For *all intents and purposes*, it's the only home *I've ever* known. And you tried to sell it. To have my abusive ex-husband sell it." She dropped her hand, let it land at her side, her voice dropping alongside it. "And if the fucked-up scheme had worked, who would get the money? You and Dad? Colt?" She laughed. "Because I know it wouldn't be me. It would *never* be me."

"Baby."

This time it wasn't shrill.

But it was manufactured all the same.

Pathetic. Destroyed. Fake tears out of Bailey's mother's eyes.

"Baby, I would never—"

"You would. You have. You would again," Bailey said. "In a heartbeat."

"I—"

Her voice was all sharp edges, all pain. "I paid you for that land." A beat. "Three years ago. I paid you." Bailey sighed. "So where did the money go?"

"I—"

"Here's the thing, *Mom*," Bailey said over her, not giving her the chance to answer, and her next words explained why. "I don't care where the money went. I don't care about Colt any longer. I don't care that you and Dad are out of money or got fucked over by some get rich quick venture again. I *don't* care."

More tears. More pathetic in her mother's voice. "You would say that to me? Your—"

"I'm going to stop you right there," I finally interjected.

Mostly because the moment that Bailey had uttered that last *I don't care*, she'd slumped against me and begun shaking.

And she'd shown her strength.

She'd proved how tough and brave she could be.

But I was done letting her carry this alone. I was down with her proving to herself that she could handle her own shit, but I wasn't cool with her shouldering this by herself. I was here. I was hers. We held hands and muddled through the shit times so that we could enjoy the good ones.

I slipped my fingers free of hers and wrapped my arm around her, tucking her close, holding her tight.

Then I turned back to her mother.

"Bailey is *mine* and I will go to any length to protect her."

A toss of her head. "That's good—"

"Let me clarify," I said. "I will protect her from you. From her shit of an ex and her useless traffic cone of a father. I will protect her from anyone who would hurt her or fuck her over or accidentally step on her goddamn pinky toe."

Flashing eyes, a venomous glare. "You—"

"She is mine," I snapped, "and I don't take kindly to people trying to fuck with what is mine." I stepped forward, bent so that my face was level with hers. "You got your money for the ranch. You got your time tonight, you have your chance to be a part of her life for twenty-five fucking years." I jabbed a finger in her direction. "But *you* fucked that up. So" —I leaned a little closer— "I am *telling* you that we're done here. *Done*. And the next time that you show your face, I *will* get the police involved."

Bailey's mom sucked in a deep breath, shoulders lifting, lungs expanding.

I held her gaze, willing her to see the intensity of my determination, and waited, ready to deal with the explosion when that air she'd sucked in was let loose.

But instead…

She surprised me, spinning on her heel and disappearing into the crowd without another word.

Bailey released a shaky breath.

"Well done, buttercup."

Her head jerked away from where her mother had disappeared, and she glanced up at me.

And then she was in my arms, her mouth on mine. I heard a crinkle, felt warm liquid gush down my side, and spared a moment of prayer for her hot cocoa (and for the fact it was no longer burning hot, but rather *warm* chocolate as it soaked into my clothes).

"Oh shit," she said, jerking back. "I'm sor—"

I just lowered my head, kissed away her apology. "It's nothing, buttercup. Nothing at all."

"I—"

"*Nothing.*"

A breath, nostrils flaring, and then she slumped against me. "Okay." Her arms came around my middle. Her forehead rested on my chest. "*Okay.*"

I smoothed a hand down her back, down along that ugly as sin sweater. "Think Billie Rose will let us off early since I need to change now?"

She lifted her head, grinned up at me. "I think Billie Rose probably has a whole wardrobe at the ready, just for this eventuality."

I laughed. "*I* think…" I kissed her nose, because it was cute and *there* and *cute*. "You're right."

A smile, finally a real one that settled my protective instincts, calmed the urge I was feeling to go after her mother and tear her to shreds.

Alas, I didn't want to go to jail.

I wanted to be right here with the woman I loved.

Though, preferably, without the side of wet shirt and pants.

She kissed my pec through the fabric. "Damn right I am." She started to straighten. "Let's find you something dry to wear."

Fingers on her cheek, sliding down, resting on the side of her throat, stilling her when she would have moved away. "Promise me that if she shows up again, you'll call the sheriff and file a report, try for a restraining order?"

"We collecting those fuckers?" she quipped.

I brushed my thumb over her pulse point. "Fuckers referring to people or the paperwork?"

A flash of white. "Either. Both."

I smiled back. "Hopefully, if we collect enough of the latter, then we can avoid the former?"

Her eyes gentled, palm smoothing over my cheek. "Still no sign of Candi?"

I shook my head. "We have the fake name, and they're scouring social media for any profiles. But right now, there's nothing that Pascal can find."

"Shit," she whispered.

"You let me handle it, okay?"

One brow lifted. "Because you're a big macho male?"

I brushed my finger over it. "Because...there's nothing more either of us can do and Pascal is already working his magic, so there's nothing to do but worry." I covered her hand with my own. "And you've got enough to worry about."

A frown. "We're supposed to—"

"Worry about pointless shit neither of us can fix at this moment?"

"Yeah. *That.*" She narrowed her eyes at me. "I'm supposed to worry and care about you."

When had I had that?

Never.

And fuck, my heart. It couldn't take this, couldn't take her, the love, her care.

"So," I said, "just to clarify, this is us agreeing that we both get to worry about pointless shit neither of us can fix?"

A brush of her lips over mine, allowing me to taste her smile. "Damn right it is."

"Collecting restraining orders like candy. Worrying for no reason." I tucked her close to my side and turned us back to the festival, waving a hand in front of us as though I were a magician about to reveal my best trick. "What's next for us?"

Now she smiled and it was warm...but it wasn't soft. It was full of that tsunami of love I felt, that maelstrom in my belly, the one ripping me from shore and propelling me right toward it again, faster than my eyes could process.

"Everything," she vowed. "What's next for us is *everything.*"

She was right.

In that moment, I just...

Didn't understand all that *everything* encompassed.

THIRTY-ONE

"I feel like we should be bringing more than just some alcohol."
I held up the twelve-pack of craft beer I'd picked up for the annual Gold holiday party—Axel was carrying two others—and was regretting not stopping at Costco.

Those pumpkin pies were delicious and huge.

A couple of them could fill up some hockey players' bellies, right?

Add in a few cans of whipped cream and call me Martha Stewart.

Axel leaned in and kissed me on the temple. "I was given strict instructions as what to bring." He gave me a lazy grin. "Apparently, without carefully detailed commands, the potluck ends up being one main course, beer, and a shit-ton of pies."

I nearly missed the step leading up onto the wide craftsman-style porch.

Carefully detailed instructions.

Right.

So maybe I wasn't anywhere in the realm of Martha.

Alas.

Oh well, I'd survive.

Hopefully with plenty of pie in my belly and an aunt who was willing to watch my mischievous dog at some point again in the near future.

Just before we'd parked, I'd gotten a text.

It was just a photograph of another chewed-up pair of heels.

Spock despised footwear that hurt women—at least, that was what I was trying to convince Billie Rose of.

She wasn't exactly impressed.

And I made a mental note to buy her a gift card as a thank you...and to replace the heels.

Grinning, I got it together and moved up the steps next to Axel, opening the door for him when we both spotted the sign taped in its center announcing to *Come Right In*.

We did.

Went right in, and stepped *right*...into chaos.

Kids were running in all directions. The conversations were a wall of noise. The people...oh God, there were a lot of them.

Holy bejeezus, there were a *lot* of people.

And none of whom I recognized.

The urge to run was strong with this one—*this one* meaning me.

But Axel didn't falter, just shifted the twelve-packs he was carrying so he had two in one hand, wrapped his other arm around me, and waded into the fold.

Tugging me along behind him.

Eeek.

People greeted him as we made our way through and they were friendly enough when he introduced me that the cacophony of sights and sounds—*and smells*, I realized—began to have less impact on my mind. I began to be able to focus more, to listen and smile and pick out which of the people were the hockey players and which were staff and which were...

Like me.

Girlfriends.

Wives.

A stutter in my heart. Maybe someday.

Eeek, indeed.

"And this is Bailey," Axel said, thankfully drawing me out of my eeeking.

I waved. "Nice to meet you, Coop," I murmured, and then when they began talking shop, I took a moment to look for some place to set the beer down.

Which Axel noticed, of course.

And apparently Coop noticed as well.

As Axel said, "We're going to find some place to go put these—"

Coop plucked the twelve-pack out of my hands. "I'll show you guys where the coolers are."

The protest that I could carry it was on the tip of my tongue.

But I was waylaid by—

"Bailey!"

Startled, I glanced down, saw the little boy from the family suite a couple of weeks ago, the one who had been having the time of his life with slime.

Today, thankfully for the state of my one nice pair of jeans, he was slime-free.

"Aiden!" I said back, bending and offering up my palm for a high five. "How's the slime making?"

He pressed his lips together, nose wrinkling.

Uh-oh.

"I got it on the carpet and Mom got mad," he grumbled.

Carpet and slime seemed like the worse combination of worlds.

"Were you supposed to take it on the carpet?"

His nose wrinkled further. "No."

"What happened?"

He was full-on scowl now. "I had to scrape the slime off with a butter knife."

I smothered my smile. "That sounds like a lot of work."

"It was." All that was missing from his pout were his crossed arms.

Curious, I asked, "Are you going to bring the slime on the carpet again?"

Now those arms crossed to complete the affect, and he sighed. "No," he muttered.

"Well then, it sounds like your mom did good parenting."

A sigh and more muttering. "Yeah."

That pout didn't fade, and call me a softy, but I couldn't take it. "Maybe you could show me how to make slime sometime?" He perked up. "I've never done it before."

"Really? Never *ever?*"

"Never *ever*," I told him solemnly.

His eyes went wide, lips parting and...

Then he screamed.

"Mom!"

I jumped, nearly fell back on my ass.

A slender blonde with a little girl propped on her hip spun, as though her superpower was somehow being able to know exactly when her kids were calling out their version of "*Mom!*"

"Bailey has never made slime." A beat. "Never *ever.*"

Her face softened as she walked over to us. "No?"

"Uh-uh."

"Well"—she tapped her chin with one manicured finger—"I guess we'll have to have another slime making day and invite Bailey."

A fist pump, no pout in sight. "Yes!"

Then he was gone, his yell of "Maddy! We're going to make *slime!*" echoing through the party.

She smiled down at me, extending her hand and helping me up.

Not that I needed it.

But the gesture was kind and warmed me in places that had long been cold.

"Thanks," I said once I was standing.

"I'm Anna."

"Bailey," I said unnecessarily.

Her blue eyes sparkled with humor. "I know." A smile. "Though not just from my son."

"Team gossip?"

"Team gossip," she affirmed. "You're as pretty as they said."

My brows drew together. I was wearing my nice jeans and a Christmas sweater that was decidedly *not* ugly—mostly because it was a deep green that I thought went with my skin tone well and that was only mostly *because* I hadn't bought it (I had Billie Rose to thank for that). Anna was...beautiful. Like one of those angel statues.

She was a woman who belonged with these men.

Sleek and slender and blond.

And wearing a black dress and heels I could never *ever*—here I smiled, sucking back the comparisons, knowing they would only drive me crazy—pull off.

"That dress is beautiful," I told her honestly.

Another smile. "Thanks." Then her expression went knowing. "Overwhelmed?"

"With this crowd?" I asked lightly.

Her eyes danced. "I think this crowd overwhelms more often than not." She leaned in, lifted a brow. "Want a pro tip?"

"Absolutely."

She widened her eyes. "Don't show fear."

Those were not the comforting words I'd expected to hear.

Anna's solemn lasted for approximately two-point-two more seconds. Then she bent over, laughter rocking her frame. "I'm just fucking with you," she managed to gasp out after a moment. "Oh God, your face." More laughter before she got it together, and I found myself chuckling alongside her, not minding being the punchline of this particular joke.

It didn't feel like she was ridiculing me.

It was...like we were all part of the joke and so it was okay to laugh about it. Laugh about this wild life and the crowd of hot hockey players and the slime-obsessed kids.

It was like...I didn't have to pass some sort of test to be welcomed in, didn't need to survive a hazing ritual. I was enough without having to make my way through the *Legends of the Hidden Temple* course, avoiding temple guards as I scrambled to collect the Life Pendants and—

I was losing my mind.

Just a little bit.

Mostly because...this was...

Nice.

So *nice* that my laughter faded, and my eyes stung.

And...

Anna slung an arm around my shoulders, turned me in the direction of the huge island that was dominating the packed kitchen. "Come on. Let's get something to eat."

———

"It's pie," I whispered approximately two minutes later, having made my way through the clusters of people (all of whom smiled and nodded or exchanged a brief greeting with me as we walked).

I was staring at the big island.

And...there was only pie.

Anna grinned.

But it was Brit who gave me the explanation. "It's tradition. Pie for dinner. Real food for dessert." She chuckled at my expression. "Comes from the first time we tried to do this. Most of the guys were single, didn't know how to bring anything but beer and chips and pies." Her smile was huge and had been plastered on many a billboard advertising a popular toothpaste brand.

My lips twitched. "So, pies for dinner?"

A shrug. "It stuck. Plus, it's Cheat Day." She reached for a knife. "So we get to go wild. And"—that smile again—"you get to go wild along with us."

"Shit," I whispered when my eyes burned, just a little bit.

"What?" she whispered back.

"You guys are too good to be true."

"No," she said gently. "We're nosy and annoying, and you'll probably be pulling your hair out before long."

"Family," I said.

"Family," she agreed. And then she grabbed a plate, slung a piece of pumpkin pie on it, and held it out to me. "But the good news?"

I nodded as I took the plate.

"New family eats first."

My lips twitched. That *was* good news. Especially considering the crowd.

A fork was tucked next to my slice of pie, and then she turned to the room, announced over the din. "All right, peeps! Soup's on!"

THIRTY-TWO

AXEL

I was in a sugar coma.

I thought I'd eaten the equivalent of one turkey breast, a dollop of mashed potatoes, and about six pieces of pie.

And Bailey was curled up next to me, watching the final showdown in *Ticket to Ride*.

"They're ruthless," she whispered, her eyes glittering with amusement when they hit mine.

"You're just saying that because you were knocked out in the first round."

"Like I said"—a grin—"they're ruthless."

"Or cheaters."

A poke to my chest. "You're just saying *that* because you got knocked out in the third round."

"No!" Mandy cried, clutching her hands to her chest and falling back on the rug.

Coop jumped up. "Fuck yeah!" Then he immediately clamped a hand over his mouth. "I mean...uh...woohoo!"

Mandy glared at him.

"You, ma'am, are just glaring because I won," he countered. "The kids have heard worse, and anyway"—he glanced over his shoulder as though double-checking his statement before he said it —"they're all watching the movie outside."

Bailey chuckled, and I took her hand, hauled her to her feet, and led her into the front room, leaving Coop and Mandy to finish up their trash talk...and clean up the board.

The winner's spoils.

Putting all the pieces back.

Grinning, I took a detour beneath the mistletoe then we found a spot on the couch. It was covered in the remnants of wrapping paper from the kids' present opening earlier that evening, and there were crumbs and empty wine glasses and mostly eaten pieces of pie all around.

I made a mental note to clear some of them so the mess wouldn't be too terrible for Brit and Stefan.

"I didn't get it," Bailey whispered. "When you talked about how they were, I thought it was total bullshit, some PR nonsense they fed the public with carefully crafted Instagram posts. But it's real. All of it." She glanced up at me. "Even the way they welcomed me. They truly *welcomed* me."

"Yeah, I know." I tucked her hair behind her ear. "No joke, it wigged me out the first time I experienced it."

She sighed, leaned into me, her hand resting on my thigh, and by the way her fingers drifted upward, tracing nonsensical patterns along the inside of my thigh, I knew she was one eggnog away from stripping down.

I should get her home.

But sitting here with the noise around us yet cocooned in our own little slice of peace, was perfection.

So, though I captured her hand, stilling the movements, I didn't get off the couch.

I just sat there with the lights of the Christmas tree glimmering around us, and I knew that I'd never had a better holiday.

Never.

A lot of it was because of this team.

Even more was because of this woman.

But the last of it, that bit had come from me.

I'd helped create this.

And that realization had a jagged piece deep in my belly filing itself smooth. That serrated spike had been buried so deep that I hadn't realized it was there still, jabbing at me. I'd thought them all long gone, all long smoothed out.

They weren't apparently.

But that one was gone now.

I breathed long and slow and deep, holding Bailey tighter when she sighed, her eyes closing as she leaned even more heavily against me.

Because she'd known.

She had understood there were still edges to me, still spikes wounding me, even though they were buried.

Entombed so deeply that I didn't know they existed.

She'd known.

And now, because of her, another had disappeared.

I glanced down to ask her if she wanted to go.

What came out instead, was "I love you."

I tucked her into the corner of the couch, covered her with a blanket.

And then I set about cleaning up some plates.

———

"Here."

I glanced from *Home Alone* down to the package she'd tossed on my bare chest.

We were on our second watch through because Bailey hadn't seen it, and we'd gotten naked halfway through the film, missing a lot of the antics, and since it was the best Christmas movie of all

Christmas movies, I had declared Bailey needed to see it from start to finish without missing any of the good stuff in between.

So, we'd started it over.

I didn't mind.

Not when it meant she cuddled close.

Not when it meant we were taking advantage of one of my last days off before I had to drive back down to San Francisco to get ready for a road trip and series of tight home and home games that would take me away from my woman for nearly two weeks.

"What's this?"

Christmas was tomorrow. We had that.

Then on Boxing Day (we had to throw a bone to our Canadian brethren), I'd drive home in the afternoon, sleep in my bed, and get my ass up early to catch the team flight.

I still couldn't believe I wasn't going to park my ass on a bus, spend hours crammed in with my teammates while driving to San Diego or Stockton or San Jose.

But I wasn't living while holding my breath, thinking that I was going to have it all ripped away from me in an instant.

I was *living*.

For now. For the future.

But none of that changed the fact that my woman had just tossed me a cheerfully wrapped package, even though it wasn't Christmas.

It wasn't time for presents yet.

And that fact had me frowning at Bailey and sitting up, capturing the package before it slid off my chest. "What are you doing, buttercup?"

A defiant look. "I'm starting a tradition."

"With presents?" I asked. "That's for tomorrow."

A shrug, a bit of pink hitting her cheeks. But her chin came up, and she gave me that tart I loved so much. "It's *my* tradition. I can do what I want."

"Or we could wait"—I glanced at my phone—"thirty-two

more minutes and it would technically be Christmas...where this tradition fits."

Now she sighed. "Why am I in love with a man who's such a pain in the ass?"

"Do you really want me to answer that?"

"Is it going to involve some innuendo about you fucking my ass?"

"Do you want me to answer *that?*"

Bailey dropped her head back, eyes on the ceiling. "Why?"

I wrapped an arm around her waist, dragged her on top of me. "You love me."

A glare in my direction—her pouty lips and wrinkled nose so fucking cute that I had to kiss her.

So I did.

And then, when we were both breathing heavy, I released her. "Should I open my present?"

"Like I've been trying to get you to do for the last ten minutes?"

"Don't make me kiss you again."

Her eyes narrowed. "Just open the present, or *I'm* going to."

I snatched it back when she reached for it. "Don't think so. It's *mine.*"

A huff.

But when I drew us both up on the bed, propped us against the headboard, she didn't complain. She didn't say much of anything, actually. I slanted a careful look her way, taking stock of her expression, the emotions in her eyes.

She was...nervous, I realized.

"Is this the moment that I should tell you the wrapping paper is ugly as sin?"

A hand on my chest, propping herself up—all the better to glare down at me.

But she knew me, knew my game.

Knew I was trying to irritate her, to get her out of her own head, and because I liked the sass, because that sass she threw my way meant that she wasn't closing down on me, wasn't locking me out of her heart, her head.

Which was why she cupped my jaw, brushed her lips over mine. "Stop worrying about me—and *my* worrying—and just open the fucking present."

I shut up.

I stopped pushing and poking and prodding (and worrying)...

And I opened the *fucking present*.

But I wasn't prepared for what was inside.

"So, you don't have to pretend that wind blew open the door," she said, referencing the first time I'd been in this house, the first time I'd gotten a glimpse of who Bailey was beneath her hard shell.

Soft and sweet and loving.

Mine.

Mine to keep, to protect, to...reveal myself to.

To give her every bit of myself.

I grabbed the key to her house, held it close to my pounding heart, feeling like the sappiest motherfucker on the planet.

But this meant *everything*.

"I'm so getting *four* drawers."

She opened her mouth, ready to give more sass...

So I kissed her.

For so long that we had to start the movie over for a third time.

Thirty-Three

I abhorred roses.

Except when Axel gave them to me.

Yup.

I was an ooey gooey puddle of slime because my boyfriend had bought me a bouquet of crimson roses...

And crimson lingerie.

And a toy.

I grinned.

I'd enjoyed that toy a whole hell of a lot before we'd gotten dressed again (and funny story, I was wearing that crimson lingerie beneath my dress...a dress that Anna had helped me pick out).

Axel and I were on a date.

A real date.

Dinner. A show. Walking around the city in an obscenely short dress and heels that I was teetering in, just a little bit.

Holding hands.

Tucked close to his side.

Of course, we'd fucked like rabbits in the hotel room *before* we'd gotten dressed up and gone out to dinner.

Out of order.

But I'd needed a shower after the long drive down—thankful that, though still into major mischief at seemingly every opportunity—Spock had lost his taste for Billie Rose's heels.

She was much more willing to watch him when she wasn't losing her footwear.

So, I'd made the drive, gotten the shower...

And Axel had needed to join me beneath the hot stream of water.

Needed.

Yup.

Now we were tucked into a shadowy corner booth, eating steaks and crab legs and chocolate cake that was sinfully rich.

And Axel's big, hot palm was drifting higher and higher up my bare thigh, finger occasionally brushing along the lace covering me.

Lace that was growing damper by the moment.

Which he knew—or felt, I supposed—considering the smirk he was wearing on that pretty, pretty face.

Just as I was getting ready to say let's forget the show and go back to the hotel for round two, I heard, "Ex-excuse me?"

We were tucked in our shadowy booth.

In a fancy restaurant.

On Valentine's Day.

But there was a teenage boy in front of us, shifting from side to side. "I'm sorry to interrupt—"

Axel slid his hand out from my dress.

"But I just wanted to see—"

An older woman came up beside him, and it only took a glance to glimpse the family resemblance between them.

"Carter," she hissed. "I told you that you could absolutely *not* come over here and bother—"

The teenager—the kid, *really*—looked ready to die a thousand deaths, right then and there, but before I could open my mouth and save him, Axel had squeezed my thigh and was up and out of the booth, extending his hand (thankfully *not* the one that had been under my dress mere moments before).

"Carter?"

The kid nodded energetically. "And you're Axel Finnegan," he breathed.

Axel smiled. "Yeah. You play?"

Another energetic nod. "Yeah. I want to be in the NHL one day."

"Keep working hard, yeah?" Axel encouraged.

"Yeah," the kid breathed, nodding vigorously.

"Want a picture?" Axel asked after a few moments where the kid just stared and seemed to forget why he'd come over.

Kid was turning into a bobblehead.

I smothered a grin, extended my hand, offering, "I'll take it if you give me your phone."

The kid's cell was in my hand an instant later and then Axel had slung his arm around Carter's shoulders, and I was taking a couple shots.

I glanced around the phone, caught his mom's eyes. "Want to get in on this one?"

Pink on her cheeks as she started to shake her head. "I—"

My smile was gentle. "It's okay," I told her. "Really."

She stepped in.

I snapped a few more shots.

Then I handed the phone back and spent the next couple of minutes chatting with Carter's mom, who spent the first half of those minutes apologizing for interrupting and then the second half of those minutes thanking me for giving Carter this time.

"It's nothing," I said. "I promise."

"Really, man?" I heard Carter exclaim. "You don't have to—"

Axel ruffled his hair. "Friday. Go to the Will Call window and tickets will be waiting for you."

The kid's smile was *huge.* "Whoa, that's awesome. Thank you."

"We should go," Carter's mom said, tugging at her son's arm. "Leave you two to your dinner."

"It's—"

But then they were gone.

I slid back into the booth. Axel slid into the other side, his body coming flush with mine.

"Was that..." I glanced around, dropped my voice. "Was that your first public recognition?"

His eyes were wide. "Yeah. I mean, *here* it was. River's Bend doesn't count because everyone knows everyone else already. But here...in the city? Yes," he whispered. "That was the first time."

"How'd it feel?"

He stilled then whispered, "I don't...actually I don't really know."

I grinned, poked his shoulder. "It felt *awesome!*" I bumped his arm with my own. "You can admit that much."

A breath, his eyes focusing. "Okay, it felt *awesome.*"

"Good." I leaned closer, nibbled at my bottom lip. "Axel?"

"Yeah?"

"I think you owe me a celebratory kiss."

Heat in his eyes. "Yeah?"

I nodded, playing a being a bobblehead myself. "Yeah."

His palm on my cheek, thumb drifting across my bottom lip, pressing down slightly. "Yeah," he murmured.

And then he kissed me.

Long and hard and with too much tongue for a restaurant... even *if* we were in a shadowy booth.

Eventually, though, we had to pull back, if only to pay our bill and leave, since our show was starting soon.

We walked to the front door, and I shivered when he helped me into my coat, sliding my hair free before he straightened the collar then bent to press a kiss to my nape.

I turned, touched his jaw. "Thanks, honey."

A half smile that sent a bolt of heat through me. I'd seen that smile when he was between my legs, smirking up at me because he'd made me come *again.*

"I love you," I whispered.

"I know."

Groaning, I let my head fall back. "You can't be quoting the wrong *Star* to me."

"*Trek, Wars,* what's the difference?"

I pretended to sputter, knowing he was just trying to irritate me. Because then he would kiss me and try to make that irritation go away (which also usually worked...both the trying to irritate *and* the disappearing of that irritation).

But I also knew him well enough to understand that he was playing.

With me.

Teasing.

Me.

Loving.

Me.

"Them's fighting words," I said playfully as we stepped out onto the street, a cold gust of wind driving me into his arms—or at least, that was what I was telling myself.

Truthfully, he was the opposite dipole of my magnet.

When we were close, I wanted to be plastered to him.

Luckily, he didn't seem to mind.

Not at that moment—when he curled his arms around me, plastering me against his body. Not ever—his arm always coming around me or his hand taking mine or his body close enough that I could feel the heat of his.

"I like your fight."

"I know," I quipped.

His mouth tipped up.

And despite his poking of the bear, despite the cold air and the holiday and our tickets to the show, I wanted to sit in what had just happened inside. "You had a fan come up to you," I whispered. "Recognize *you*. Want to be *you*."

"It wasn't—"

I stopped him before he could demure further, rising on tiptoe and pressing a finger to his lips. "It was about you. *You.*" I cupped his cheek. "And you deserve it, honey," I told him earnestly. "I am *so fucking* proud of you."

"Buttercup—"

"You," I repeated. "I am proud of *you.*"

He inhaled sharply.

And I took advantage, pressing my lips to his, accepting the hard kiss he gave me in return, feeling all the emotion he was pouring into it, into me, into *us*.

"You," I said again when he released me.

His eyes were a little glassy, but he just smoothed his thumb over my lip, spun me so my side was tucked into his, and wrapped his arm around me.

Keeping me close.

Loving me.

I smiled, rested my head on his arm, content to just walk beside him.

Content until we turned a corner and I caught a flash of blond, of something familiar...*someone* familiar.

"You good?"

I didn't realize I'd stopped, not until Axel cupped my cheek, tilted my head up.

"I'm fine. I just—"

I glanced back.

Just a crowd.

Not one familiar face.

Shaking myself, I smiled up at the man I loved. "Let's get this show over with." My smile turned wicked. "So, we can go back to the hotel, and I can give you *my* show."

THIRTY-FOUR

AXEL

"We've got a hit on Facebook," Pascal told me. "Her full name is Candice Walters."

Candice Walters.

That sounded respectable.

It didn't sound like a buxom blonde with a penchant for glitter who'd spied on me while I fucked a woman and then later had broken into my hotel room and tried to separate me and Bailey.

I didn't know her.

And she'd somehow fashioned in her mind that we should be together.

Which was crazy and dangerous and had *hurt* Bailey.

So, Pascal getting a hit on Candi's real name, him getting me one step closer to being able to keep a record of that crazy, to file a restraining order that would hopefully stop her from wanting to come around me was a good thing.

"Won't be long now," Pascal said. "And if the restraining order doesn't deter any future interactions...I'll have a word with her."

I didn't know what that word was, nor what it might be.

I only knew that it would be scary.

I only knew that it would certainly convince her to keep her distance if she ignored the restraining order.

"Thanks." I leaned back against the wall of his office, the space surprisingly messy—including his single visitor's chair, which was full of papers and files. Forcing my gaze from that, I held his stare. "I mean that, and I want to pay—"

"No thanks needed," he said. "And you gave me a deposit so I could pay my guys. We go over that, I'll let you know."

"I—"

"You gonna argue with me about keeping your woman safe, son?"

"You need to be compensated—"

"I have plenty of money. But a good job, good people—" A pause that said...well, more than Pascal usually ever said. "I'm good." His eyes sliced through me. "And I'll let you know when I'm not."

No lie, that sent a little shiver of fear down my spine.

Because...Pascal was scary.

But luckily for me, all that scary was currently being used for my good.

"Okay."

"Okay."

I might have thought that was a dismissal, except for the fact that Pascal had asked me to meet him in his office after practice to discuss two things.

Candi was one.

The other—

Pascal picked up a folder, opened it. "I just got word from my guy up in River's Bend. Colt hasn't been seen around town at all since Bailey and him had their *chat*"—which was a nice euphemism for Bailey's sign wielding, along with Pascal's threatening (both of which I would have paid to have seen)—"and word has it that he's moved up to Eureka since he's no longer working for Garret Smothers. Trying to start his own real estate company."

The inflection on trying told me that it hadn't been successful and that it probably wouldn't be.

But there was distance between my woman and that man.

And I couldn't give two fucks about the bastard, so long as he kept well away.

"I'll keep regular tabs on him, but—for now—with Colt gone and Candi nearly run to ground, it's probably safe to pull my guy off Bailey in River's Bend."

I didn't like that.

It was logical.

Pascal was the expert in this situation.

But my woman...

I didn't like the term *probably* safe.

Pascal's mouth curved as he closed the file and set it on a teetering stack. "We'll keep him there for another week."

"You don't have to."

"Another week." And *that* was a dismissal. So, I didn't protest, just nodded, gave him another "Thanks" that I knew he was going to ignore since gratitude made him uncomfortable, and hit the hallway.

"Axel."

I turned and I couldn't help the nerves that immediately began swirling in my belly. Authority did that to a person who cared, and the man standing in the hall ten feet behind me was the ultimate authority for the Gold.

Pierre Barie.

Stefan's father.

Brit's father-in-law.

And the boss of all my bosses because he owned the Gold and the Rush.

So, yeah, even though I'd been playing well and producing, and the scoresheet had my name on it more often than not (and not just because I was spending all my time sitting in the penalty box), the nerves still hit me, hard and fast and *intense*.

"Mr. Barie."

"Pierre."

Yeah, that wasn't going to happen, though I nodded in agreement, not about to argue with the boss of all my bosses.

The silence stretched.

And all the while my stomach churned as I waited.

The last time I'd seen this man, he'd hijacked my workout from hell—*hell* because I'd been putting myself through the wringer, trying to avoid Bailey, and more importantly trying to avoid what I *felt* about Bailey.

The last time I'd seen this man, he'd told me I'd had potential, had fire for the game, for my career, for my future...and I'd pissed it all away.

The last time I'd seen this man, he'd made it clear that he saw I could find that fire again.

And I had.

But was it not enough?

So even if I wanted to speak, wanted to find the words, I knew I couldn't open my mouth.

I might vomit on his shoes. Hell, my throat was so dry, my tongue felt so swollen that I didn't think it could actually help me form words.

Thankfully, he didn't need me to.

After that long, intense moment of quiet, he broke the silence.

"You found it."

Three words, but they freed my throat, shrank my tongue. "I found *her*."

Twinkling blue eyes. "You found her, and she led you back to it."

I'd worked my ass off to get here. I *still* worked as hard as I could, tried to take advantage of every opportunity and advantage and bit of help, training, and coaching that came my way.

But there was absolutely not one fucking bit of doubt in my mind that if not for Bailey, I wouldn't be here.

"Yes," I agreed.

Solemn blue eyes, studying me like he could see into the depths of my very soul. Maybe he could. Maybe that was his fucking superpower, or maybe the fact that I loved Bailey with every single part of my being was just so fucking obvious to every other person on the planet that it wasn't hard to see.

To know what was driving me.

To understand it wasn't because Bailey wanted me to be successful in the league, wasn't that she wanted to date a professional hockey player, wanted to be with someone who made a lot of money or was on TV and the occasional billboard (and slightly more than occasional online ad) selling underwear.

I was here, now, because Bailey had made me *see*.

That I wasn't my past, even though the mistakes riddling it were vast, were awful, made me more than a bit of an asshole.

That I wasn't my mother, who made my mistakes, my multitude of fuckups seem like they were equivalent to winning a Nobel Prize.

That I wasn't defined by what I did on the ice, or even what I did when I was off it.

I was...a culmination of all those things.

But more importantly, more impactful than that entire list of all the things I wasn't, she saw that it was who I was inside that defined me.

Not the asshole who was afraid to let anyone get close, lest I get hurt.

But the man inside, who craved someone I could call mine, craved a place in a family that was healthy and loving, even if that family wasn't related by blood.

Me.

What I needed.

Who I was beneath the shield.

Me.

And that man, stripped of barriers and shields and protective asshole insulation, was enough.

Just me.

Pierre patted me on the shoulder.

"Welcome back."

THIRTY-FIVE

BAILEY

I t was my third hockey game. Ever.

And it was like I was a newbie all over again.

Not that the two previous games I'd gone to made me an expert, but it was a completely new experience rooting for the *away* team.

And doing it while watching *playoff* hockey.

I wasn't sitting in the Gold Mine.

I wasn't surrounded by fans rooting for *my* players.

In fact, I was a shining gold gem in a sea of teal, easily picked off by the ocean of San Jose fans. I'd better watch out and keep my shouts of encouragement to myself, otherwise the foam board shark teeth cut-out a pair of teenage girls were wielding behind my head might come for me.

The lights dimmed and the players darted out onto the ice, skating a couple of laps, rolling their shoulders, lining up for the anthem.

It was loud—cheers filling the older arena.

But—I smirked to myself—not as loud as the Gold Mine.

That noise had my ears hurting, the screams having me consider earplugs. These were...meh. Good.

Just not as good as *my* boys.

Though, of course, I may be biased.

Okay, I *was* biased, especially as I watched Axel complete his laps and take his place on the bench. He was the prettiest and most talented hockey player of all time. *Right*. Now I actually let my smirk free as they all took their positions. He was *my* big, broody hockey player and *I* thought he was the best ever.

Mentally, I shrugged.

Perspective.

I had *one* of them.

And the fact that I got to go home and fuck him? That I got to go home and *love* him?

Small details.

Best. *Ever*.

Grinning, I stood as the lights overhead grew bright and saw the carpet rolled out near the boards, a teal-jersey-wearing singer already holding the microphone and waiting for her cue to belt out the anthem.

The music went.

She sang.

The crowd cheered, adding a few good-natured "You suck!" calls during the second verse...as one did (though I didn't love when Finnegan got his turn).

But then the anthem was over.

The crowd was sitting.

And the puck had been dropped.

It was intense, even more than the game I'd made it to a few weeks back. I'd wanted to come to more—and had watched nearly every game Axel played in, at least on TV—but the schedule was tough, and Axel preferred that if I drove down, we actually spent time together. Not just a few stolen hours in the evening before I had to go home, or he needed to go to practice. But *actual* time together that didn't have thousands of people, ice, and glass between us.

So, we took advantage of his days off.

But this was probably going to be the last game I could make it to for a while.

The cows were almost ready to go to market.

Not just for me, but for all my neighbors. The next few weeks would be a flurry of work for me up at the various ranches in River's Bend and, if Axel and the Gold managed to keep winning, their work wouldn't stop either.

This was crunch time for both of us.

But Axel and the guys needed to just focus on one game at a time.

I crossed my fingers, heart in my throat, and tried to breathe. This was only game one in the series. There was still lots of time for the matchup to go either way, so there were plenty of opportunities, even if they did lose tonight, for the guys to win four games and move on. But the stakes were higher, and my body knew that, was pumping me full of nerves and adrenaline.

If that was happening to *me*, I could hardly fathom what the actual players were going through.

Give me manure and repairing fencing every single day.

"Ooh!" the crowd said, and I winced at the hit Coop took along the boards.

The *boom* from the contact was loud enough to reach my ears even over the noise and I held my breath as Coop got up, the boards still shaking, the glass rocking back and forth in a way that seemed like it was going to fall out from the metal holders on both sides. But get up Coop did, hardly missing a step as he sprinted up the ice, joining in the play.

And seriously, *give me cow shit* any day of the week.

———

I groaned when San Jose scored.

Cheered when the Gold got one back.

Clenched my hands together when Brit took on and shut down a breakaway.

Cheered again when Axel's line scored (and he made a beautiful pass—see? My hockey knowledge was improving).

And then clutched my hands back together as the game went back and forth, good scoring opportunities to be had on both ends of the ice.

The final buzzer went off, and the teams circled up near their benches, players patting each other on the backs before heading back to their respective locker rooms.

I finally breathed...then cheered my freaking head off.

Because the Gold had won, two to one.

Axel glanced up at me, smiled that special smile, the one that was just for me.

My heart squeezed as I smiled back and watched him disappear into the bowels of the arena. I didn't bother standing, didn't worry about winding my way through the departing crowd. I stayed seated, waiting in my seat for a while, knowing it would take a bit for the fans to disperse out the exits, to get in their cars and drive home. Just like it would take a while for Axel to finish what he needed to after the game—media requests, cooldown, shower.

He'd meet me when that was all done.

And it sometimes took a while.

Not that I minded.

I was content to be here, to give him something back when he'd given me so much.

I waited until the rows around me were empty then made my way up the stairs and into the concourse, pit stopping in the now uncrowded bathroom before making my way to my own exit.

He'd take the bus back to the Gold's practice facility and pick up his car.

I'd be in his bed by then.

Naked.

And I really wouldn't be sad with the way he woke me up.

I was speaking from personal experience...of his tongue and fingers and cock.

Heh.

My smile hurt my cheeks as I exited the arena and headed to my own vehicle, unlocking the doors and starting to get in when I saw the scrap of paper on my windshield.

I snagged it, frowned when all that was written on it was *Bitch.*

Well, I supposed I *had* parked pretty close to the line on the passenger side.

Either that or the Gold license plate holder that Axel had given me a few weeks back hadn't been appreciated after they'd beat the home team that night.

Shrugging, I balled the note, shoved it into the cubby in the driver's side door then hefted myself up into Gramps's truck.

I drove to Axel's apartment.

I got naked.

And...he woke me up in the most glorious way ever.

———

I went back to River's Bend the following morning, Spock and Billie Rose greeting me in the driveway with kisses—both on my cheeks, one albeit much more wet.

I sorted the ranch and my chores.

Axel and the Gold got back to work.

And as the days wore on and my knee-deep adventure in cattle, manure, and getting calves and heifers and steers ready for market began, the Gold *kept* winning.

The first round—four games to three.

The second—four to one.

The third—four to three.

And finally, they sailed into the fourth and final round, the Cup within grasp. The series was brutal, the teams tied two games to two.

And that...

That was when everything fell apart.

Thirty-Six

AXEL

I 'd gotten used to the pressure.
Kind of.
It was...not exactly bearable.
But I was tolerating it well enough.
Or had been.

After tonight though? My body was tired. I was sore from head to toe, and ibuprofen, massages, and ice baths were my best friends of late.

But I didn't have any major injuries.

Rome was playing with a broken thumb, Coop had a sprained back, Ethan was sporting a bruise the size of a locomotive on his ribs. Blue had a stress fracture in his ankle, Ben had stitches on his arm from an errant skate blade. Brit had tweaked her groin.

Logan, Kayden, Josh, and the rest of the team were in my camp —healthy, but tired, sore, and trying to focus on the goal within our grasp.

The Cup was close.

We needed to win two more.

Because we'd lost tonight, and for the first time in the playoffs, we were down in a series.

Now we were in a sudden death situation—win or it was all over, and we had to do it on the road, away from our support system, our normal routines, our families.

Christ.

This sucked.

I was tired, so damned tired.

I wanted to be done.

I wanted—

A bump on my shoulder had me glancing up, looking into Brit's milk chocolate eyes. She'd played well tonight, but had left the game early.

"How's the groin?"

A shrug. "Everything hurts at this point in the season," she said. "But we'll survive."

"Yeah."

Another nudge. "You played good tonight," she said. "One of the few of us who did."

"You—"

She handed me a towel. "I'm giving you a compliment."

I wiped the sweat from my face, grunting softly in answer.

"Thanks, Brit, you played great, too," she said in a rough—and terrible—approximation of my voice. "We couldn't do it without you." Still in a rough voice. "We couldn't do *anything* without you."

I chuckled despite myself. "It's funny because it's true," I told her.

She tossed me one of her award-winning smiles. "I know."

I slung the towel around my neck. I needed to summon up my energy, to get in the shower, get home, get some rest.

All the gets.

Bailey might still be up if I hurried up and got my shit together.

But I didn't move.

I felt...off.

Wrong.

"You know," Brit said. "I've had a lot of coaches in my life."

I slanted a look her way, lifted my brows.

We'd *all* had a lot of coaches by the time we made it to the Big Show. Dozens of them, at least. Maybe more than that if I considered them all from the time I first began playing.

"Yeah," I prompted when she didn't go on.

"But I had one that really stood out."

I waited.

Prompted her with "Yeah" again when she didn't fill in the rest of the blanks for me.

"He was an asshole most of the time, old, crotchety as fuck, and had gotten his PhD in screaming."

That sounded familiar.

"Occasionally, though, he gave us a gem to hold on to, something that made me not hate his guts, at least for a few moments."

"Are you about to impart to me one of those gems?"

"Ding. Ding. Ding." She tapped her nose. "Got it in one."

"And that gem is?"

"Flush it away."

She'd given me that advice once, way at the beginning of the season, when I was just squeaking out an occasional game in the big leagues.

And I'd flushed the bullshit way.

"I remember that."

A lifted brow. "You sure about that?"

"I think I'd remember hockey advice packaged as a toilet analogy."

She grinned. "Okay, that's fair. But that's not the entirety of the gem I wanted to share."

Heaven help me.

"Hit me," I ordered.

"Flush it away." I nearly groaned. "Or sit in the pile of shit forever."

"How poetic," I muttered.

She laughed. "That was Coach. A poet, right down in his cold, dead heart." A beat. "But he was right about it. We either sit in our own misery, sit in our own shit, or we flush it down the drain." That *poetry* was accompanied by a jaunty bend of her finger, mimicking the flushing of a toilet, and hell if I didn't laugh.

Which earned me another bump.

"Take a breath, flush it down, regroup." She stood. "Trust the process and refocus for the next game. We'll get them."

"How do you know?"

A pat to her sweat-clad legs. "I feel it in these old bones."

Snorting, the idea of her, a woman in her thirties, calling herself old—especially one who played as well as she did, even if retirement was in her future—was absurd.

But her grin told me she knew it was absurd.

So did her pat on my knee. "Flush it down, and put these young bones to work. Keep doing what you're doing and..."

"Flush the bad stuff down."

"Yes!" A beat. "But, also, no." She crouched a little so that we were eye to eye, her standing, me sitting. "We got this, yeah?" Her eyes went to mine, held for a long moment, and then she repeated, "Yeah?"

Her belief slid through me, curled around my mind, my heart, my *belly*.

And I knew we had it too.

"Yeah," I agreed.

"That's fucking *right*." A punch to my shoulder before she straightened, turned away, though not before tossing over her shoulder. "But for fuck's sake, *Balls,* take a goddamned shower. You stink."

Then she was gone.

And so used to the nickname—rendered from my Harvest Festival crystal ball fortune-telling self—I ignored it.

I didn't ignore her advice, though.

Just stood up, stripped down, and got my ass into the shower.

After, smelling much cleaner (and theoretically now up to Brit's smell standards), I went back to my locker and started getting dressed.

Underwear. Socks. Pants. Shirt. Shoes.

Except as I shoved my foot into my shoe, something crinkled.

Which was...weird as fuck.

I toed it off, reached my hand in, and tugged out the small piece of paper. It was a crumbled label for...a type of lotion?

Weird.

But the guys used weird shit all the time.

Even—I took one more glance at the label before crumpling it up and tossing it in the trash—lotion with glitter in it.

Probably something that found its way from one of the guys' kiddos or wives.

Likely it had been bandied around the room while I'd been giving interviews or had been balled up and launched at someone's head, starting shit...or ending it...or just blowing off some steam pre- or post-game.

Either way, that glitter lotion bullshit was now in the trash.

And my feet were in my shoes, minus the crinkling.

I shrugged into my jacket, slid on my belt, pocketed my cell and wallet, noting on the former that Bailey had ordered me to text her, no matter how late.

I sighed.

Flush the B.S. away.

Refocus and regroup.

I tugged out my cell, sat back down on the bench.

The room was empty, and it was late. Bailey had to get up early. I shouldn't bother her, shouldn't keep her up any later. But I still unlocked my phone and hit her contact anyway. I told myself that it was to put her at ease earlier than if I waited to call until I got to my car or until I made it home. That calling her *now* was better for her.

But it was better for me.

Because I knew of no easier way to get my head sorted, to flush it all down, than to talk to my woman.

The phone rang.

Bailey picked up before it rang a second time. "Hey, honey," she said gently.

And...I was right.

That soft *honey* had the shit flushed right down.

Not even five seconds and she got my head straight.

Thirty-Seven

Bailey

Hot coffee. Cold air.
A pupper at my side.
Cattle to be sorted.

But the trucks would be here soon, and my calves would be loaded first, then the extra heifers and steers that I couldn't afford to feed any longer would make it on the next truck. Both would still bring a good profit, especially since all of our neighboring ranches had pooled our resources and herds so that we saved on transport costs, shared expenses, and got a better deal at the auction.

This year we were trying for two trips to market.

Our normal late spring and one in December to take advantage of the increasing frequency of off-season calves and the changing California weather—shorter winter, warmer months.

Go us.

Marketing extraordinaries who were hustling-hustling (and yes, I sang that in my head every time I thought about it).

We weren't big ranches, but together we brought a decent

haul, and if we were smart, that haul meant we were all set for the year. A second auction would just be icing on the cake...and hopefully my ticket to paying off the last of the second mortgage and go toward tuition for my credentials and hiring someone to take over the brunt of the ranch duties so I could actually attend classes.

I told Axel I'd find a way.

I had.

I was just lucky that my neighbors were on board and willing to take advice from a woman who was relatively new to the business.

Though, Tommy and Hank and Eli knew me, had known my grandparents, and I'd earned their respect these last years, earned the right to propose something, earned the right to try something new, earned the right to run the ranch like Gramps might have.

But just right then, I was sitting on my porch, thinking about cows and Axel and my life.

So different from what I'd planned.

And I was still happy.

Smiling, I sipped my coffee, feeling settled in a way I had never expected. Part of that came from handling my own shit—airing out shit with my mom, confronting Colt, sorting out my finances so that I had a full fridge and didn't have to subsist solely on sandwiches and hard work, planning for the future. But the rest of it came from having a person in my life who treated me like an equal.

I didn't have to agree with everything Axel said, didn't have to walk on tiptoe or hide parts of myself or be hurt.

We were equals.

And...he had turned to me when he needed me, wanting to hash out the tough game from a couple of nights ago, needing me to help him get his head sorted.

That had—

Well, there had been a lot of moments with Axel that I could pinpoint where I might have fallen in love with him if I hadn't already been in deep, hadn't already passed over my heart to him.

I just...

Didn't expect them to keep coming, to keep falling in love with him deeper and deeper.

It was more than I expected, more than I'd ever hoped for.

I was happy. I was settled. I was standing on my porch wanting him to be there, but knowing that us being apart was okay, too.

Look at me, being all sappy at a quarter to five in the morning.

Grinning, I brought my mug back inside, Spock trailing me as I took my mug to the sink, setting it inside, and heard the sound of the trucks approaching, smiling when I thought that perhaps the anticipation, the adrenaline already flowing, the way my body went into an instant ready mode might be a little like what Axel experienced before he jumped on the ice.

I'd have to ask him.

But later.

Because gravel was crunching.

My neighbors were rolling in. We had cattle we needed to sort and get on a truck.

It was my version of game time

It was go time.

———

The water was still running brown.

I was standing in the shower, letting the water flow over me, trying to summon the energy to reach for the loofa and add some soap to the party.

So far, that battle hadn't been won.

I was just under the warm stream of water, letting it soothe my sore, overworked muscles and congratulating myself on a day that had gone well.

It was done. The trucks were loaded. The calves and culled heifers and bulls were all off to auction.

We could breathe.

For a few moments anyway.

Smiling, I snatched the loofa, loaded it with soap, and set about cleaning myself of the layers of dirt.

It took a while, but in the end, I was clean and smelling like my normal apple-scented self.

I managed the energy to shampoo and condition my hair then sat in the hot water for just a few more minutes because it felt so freaking good.

Then I dried off and slapped some moisturizer on my face and moved into the bedroom.

Pajamas.

Text Axel to let him know I was done.

Then sleep...for a thousand years. Or until tomorrow, when I vegged out, did the bare minimum around the ranch, and then cuddled up on my couch with copious amounts of snacks to watch Axel kick some hockey ass.

Grinning, I scratched Spock's ears then turned to the dresser, started to tug open my drawer, intent on my pajamas, but stopped, my fingers on the handle. I didn't want to wear my boring tank and shorts. I wanted to wear something that belonged to my man.

I said that to myself as though it were a new thought.

But really, I'd been having this little battle—pretending like I should wear my clothes then stopping and opening up Axel's drawer, tugging out one of his shirts and wearing it instead—for weeks now.

Long enough that I'd started to deplete his supply of tees.

Well—I mentally shrugged—I guess tomorrow would be laundry day.

My lips twitched. If could lift my arms that was.

So maybe the next day.

Laughing to myself, I tugged open the drawer, snagged a tee, one of the few that were left in the back.

But as I was tugging it out, it caught on something.

Frowning, I bent closer, yanked a little harder, saw the edge of a...folder?

Which was weird, but I was tugging hard now, until I was a little worried about ripping the shirt, but whether it was autopilot or just fatigue seeping into my mind and making it hard for me to shift tasks, I didn't know. All I understood was that it was like my body had taken over my brain and I couldn't stop, couldn't let the shirt go, close the drawer, and put on my own pajamas.

Instead, I'd started pulling and I couldn't let it go, not until it was free.

I wanted the shirt.

I needed it.

And...I had it.

The shirt suddenly came free, and I'd been pulling so hard that I stumbled back a few feet, nearly fell right onto my ass.

But the tee wasn't the only thing that suddenly came free.

The folder did too.

And papers flew...everywhere.

"Fuck," I whispered, tugging the shirt over my head before squatting down, intent on gathering up the papers, putting them back in the folder. I'd explain to Axel. I'd apologize. I'd—

I froze.

Because during my fretting, I'd already snagged most of the papers, was stacking them up, but then I actually saw what they were.

Saw that they were a real estate valuation.

Of my ranch.

In my house. My dresser. *My* drawer.

No. They were in *Axel's* drawer.

Axel had a real estate evaluation in his drawer.

After everything—after I'd shared how important the ranch was to me, to my grandparents, to my future, after the bullshit with Colt, after these *months* together, giving him everything I was, everything I hope to be—he had a valuation for selling *my* ranch in one of the drawers I'd given him.

I'd given *him.*

Hurt was a blistering firestorm through me, burning my insides, my throat, the backs of my eyes.

But I didn't cry.

Couldn't cry.

I just let that hurt burn through me, scald me, and set fire to all the pain seeing those papers created.

I was too tired, too weak, and then thankfully, too...numb to cry.

So, I curled up in my bed.

Spock curled up next to me.

And I slept.

THIRTY-EIGHT

AXEL

I hadn't heard from Bailey the night before, but I tried not to worry.

She'd warned me the day would be long and that she might not have the time to talk at the end of it.

I'd figured she'd text me though.

We always texted before we went to bed, even if it was a quick, *I'm home. I'm thinking of you. Night*, kind of thing.

But last night.

Nothing.

And I hadn't wanted to text her, hadn't wanted to risk waking her up if she was sleeping.

She worked too hard as it was.

I was in a hotel room, alone, and clearly the one of us with more time on our hands, at least for the moment.

So, I was watching TV, trying not to worry, and killing time before we took the bus to the arena.

And finally, *finally*, she FaceTimed me.

"Thank God," I whispered, shutting off the TV, and answering the call.

The video came through and I'd already been smiling, but one glance of her face had my smile fading.

"What is it?" I asked quickly. "Are you okay?"

The silence, the pause...they both killed me.

Then she held up a paper. "Why is there a real estate valuation hidden in the back of your drawer?"

My gut clenched.

Hard, fast, tight.

Painful knots that stole my words at exactly the wrong time. What I should have been doing was explaining immediately that I had it done way before we'd had a conversation about her needing to figure out her finances and the ranch on her own. What I should have told her was that I'd had it done before we'd had our conversation about how important the ranch was to her in terms of her grandparents and her family heritage (her parents excluded).

But all I could do was swallow hard, clear my throat, and die slowly, painfully inside while the words slowly, painfully died in the back of my throat before they could make it to my tongue.

"I can't believe you did this to me," she whispered, and the quiet, shaking words sliced through me.

A thousand slices.

A hundred punches to my gut.

"You really have nothing to say to me?" she whispered.

And that, finally, shook off the fog, loosened my throat. "Bailey." Except, that was as far as I got, was as far as I managed before my words stoppered up, before I stood there like a useless pile of crap.

She paused, waited for me to talk, to say more than her name.

I didn't.

I couldn't.

Then she shook her head, sighed, and the look flashing across her face...

I'd hurt her. I wasn't doing anything about it, wasn't fixing it. I wasn't any better than her ex, her parents. I wasn't—

Going to do *this*.

"Wait," I blurted when I saw her finger moving to the bottom of the screen, knowing she was going to end the call. "Just. Please. Let me explain."

Her hand dropped back to her side, but she didn't say anything, didn't reply.

Just waited.

Like I'd asked.

I inhaled, released it slowly. "I had that done months ago. Right after I found out about the second mortgage."

She didn't respond.

"I—then we had that conversation at Cole's ranch, you talked to me about what Russet Ranch meant to you, and I knew the report wouldn't matter. I just put it out of my mind, didn't pursue it." I shook my head as my phone buzzed, telling me it was almost time to head down for the bus. "But I didn't cancel it. I'd already paid the real estate agent for her time, and I figured even though you weren't going to sell, it would be good information for you to have, to know how much it's worth now."

"So why didn't you show it to me?"

"Because I got it back shortly after all the shit went down with Colt trying to list your place. I wasn't going to talk about it with you then—"

"Why?"

The sharp question had me freezing again, my throat struggling to allow words through.

"I didn't want you to think I was pushing you to sell, especially after you'd dealt with Colt." I cleared my throat. "And because I'd forgotten I even asked for it until it was delivered, and then since I was heading out on the road, I just threw it into the bag I was packing. It was a big one, 'cause I had to fill up the drawers you'd given me." I tried for a smile, but her face didn't change.

She just lifted a hand, rubbed her forehead. "I don't know why you hid it."

I'd come home, grabbed the bag, gotten into my car, and immediately headed up to Bailey.

I hadn't been thinking about the valuation.

I hadn't been thinking about anything except getting to Bailey.

"I wasn't thinking," I admitted. "I just made a pit stop to grab the duffle and went up to see you."

"But you hid it in the back of the drawer."

"I didn't hide it."

She dropped her hand, lifted her brows.

"I was unpacking and I came across it and you'd had a shit week and I wasn't going to bring up a sore subject about something that didn't matter."

"Axel," she sighed.

"And because I didn't want you to think that I was trying to pressure you to sell."

She was quiet, for a long, long time.

"Buttercup?"

A breath, and then she rubbed her forehead again. "I need to think about this."

"Bailey, honey—"

"We're supposed to be partners. You're supposed to be my equal, to share stuff, not to hide it and—"

"Trust me," I said, and my phone buzzed again with the reminder that I needed to get downstairs, to catch the bus to the arena. "Please just...*trust* me. Look at the dates. Look and read the report—"

"I read every word."

"Buttercup."

"I *read every word.*"

She sighed and though her voice was soft, the pain in it cut right through me. "I have...I've trusted you, trusted you with everything I ever was and ever hope to be and I trusted you with *me.* I trusted you to do the same, to share the same, not to keep things from me because you need to protect me, because you don't think I can handle—"

"Bailey, that's not it at all," I protested. "You're one of the strongest people I know. You're my partner. Please don't doubt that for a moment."

"This—" A shake of her head. "I need time."

"Please, honey. Please just—"

There was a knock at my door.

I glanced up.

"This is—"

"Time to go, motherfucker!" Logan yelled through the door.

She sighed. "This is shit timing," she whispered. "I'm sorry. You have a game you need to focus on. An important one. I shouldn't have done this now, not when you're playing for the fucking *Stanley Cup.*"

"You're more important," I said.

And meant it.

She was, and there would never be a moment in my life when I doubted it.

"Honey," she whispered.

"Wakie wakie, Balls!" Logan yelled. "Time to get pumped!"

I ignored him. "Bailey—"

"This is your dream, Axel." A breath that rattled through the speakers. "This"—she held up the papers—"can wait. It can all wait. Focus on the game. We'll talk tomorrow."

This was my nightmare.

I didn't want to talk to her tomorrow.

I wanted to erase the hurt from her eyes. Right then.

"You're right," I said. "You're right that I should have just told you. I'm so sorry. I—"

One more knock.

"Go," she whispered.

"Buttercup."

"I'm fine. *We're* fine. I'm sorry, too." But she didn't sound fine. She didn't look fine. I didn't *feel* fine. "This isn't the time. We'll talk tomorrow."

"We should talk now."

"Axel. Go, honey. We'll talk tomorrow."

Not one edge of soft in her tone. Not one opening that I could see in her face.

Just hurt.

"I love you," I whispered.

"Tomorrow," she whispered back.

And then she hung up.

Thirty-Nine

I sighed as I reined Data in.

It was just me, Picard, and Spock on the ranch (and two hundred head of cattle). My boarding horses had been gone for the last week with their owners on a long trip out of state and wouldn't be back for a couple more weeks.

So today, it was just me and my animals and the ranch.

Just me, in my life, and not struggling for a change.

Not financially.

Not stuck in an abusive relationship.

Not dragged down by my family.

I had friends, was building my own family, and I'd picked the worst time ever to throw a wrench into my life, to do my level best to implode it.

Why had I confronted Axel earlier that morning?

I should have just waited until he was in town and we were together to bring it up.

I should have waited until the series was over.

I sighed.

I had shit timing.

Mostly because I knew that me thinking I should have waited to confront him meant that I was thinking I should have done exactly what he *had* done.

I wanted to protect him. *Should* have protected him.

And it wouldn't have been lying to him or thinking that he couldn't handle the tough stuff in our lives. It wouldn't have been thinking he wasn't my equal.

It would have been choosing the right time to talk to him.

Instead of going zero to a hundred, not thinking of the consequences, and barreling through.

Fucking our relationship up, dumping shit on him when he was on the other side of the country and unreachable and playing one of the biggest games of his career.

And I'd barreled. I'd fucked up. I hadn't thought or loved or protected.

I was his girlfriend. I should be thinking of ways to make his life easier, just like he did for me all the fucking *time*.

"Shit," I muttered.

God. I was such an idiot.

And I couldn't call him. He wouldn't have his phone. The players weren't allowed to have them this close to game time.

I still tugged my cell out of the saddle bag and sent him a text anyway.

Because I was an idiot. Because I wanted him to know that, to know I was sorry.

Because he'd told me he loved me, and *I'd* told *him* that I would talk to him tomorrow.

The last time I'd done something this stupid, had run off without thinking, it had bought me a four-hour tear-filled drive with my parents and ex waiting for me at the end of it.

This time...

I might have really fucked up Axel's headspace.

And that might mean that I'd really fucked up his game, his team, his career...the close family he was building.

"Fuck," I whispered, wanting him to text back, to see my message and feel better about the fight, hoping he wouldn't hold my idiocy against me, even though I knew he couldn't see my text, wouldn't for a while, knew that he wouldn't be able to respond.

So, I was riding around the ranch on Data, Spock at my side, and sitting in my misery.

But now I was back at the barn.

I was at the house with all its reminders.

I was watching my adorable—and still mischievous—pup, watching the puppy *Axel* had given to me run circles around Data, yipping as he chased bugs, stuffing his nose into the gaps of the fencing to check out Picard, who mooed back in greeting.

And their antics made me feel a little better.

I'd find a way to make it right.

And Axel would be okay. He was a professional, just one piece in a tapestry of other professionals. He'd put me out of his mind.

He'd focus.

He'd play some hockey and tomorrow we'd talk and—

It would all be okay.

——

It wasn't okay.

He was a mess.

Christ.

Nothing was working.

Passes were off, shots were blocked or went wide. He'd even fallen in the middle of the ice, when no one was even near him.

But more than that, I could see it in his eyes.

See that he wasn't there.

I'd done that.

Fuck.

And I was trapped on the other side of the country, fucking hamstringed from being able to help him, and I couldn't do jack shit but watch him struggle, watch him hurt, watch his game play get worse and worse and *worse* as the period went on.

And it wasn't just affecting him.

It was affecting the entire team.

My fault. My fault. My—

Fucking hell. *Fucking*—

My gaze caught on my cell, sitting on the coffee table, the screen black. Billie Rose had called earlier, asking if I wanted to go into town, but I had put her off, claiming fatigue for yesterday. Thankfully, she'd bought my excuse and had left me to my own devices, aka misery.

I wished I could talk to Axel, could apologize.

Could make it right so that he could start kicking some hockey ass.

But I couldn't hop on a plane and get there in time, couldn't get in my car and drive to the arena, couldn't do anything but watch my boyfriend fall apart on national television.

"Fuck," I whispered, picking up my phone, scrolling through.

As though me looking through my messages might actually make a bit of difference, might change something.

But there was nothing.

Just my text from that afternoon. Axel's from the day before.

And a long chain from a few days before with several of the women from the Gold, trying to organize a girl's night that worked with everyone's schedules—Brit, Anna, Calle, Mandy—

Wait.

Mandy.

Brit was on the ice.

Anna was home with her and Blue's kiddos.

Calle was on the bench, coaching the team my actions were threatening to implode.

But Mandy...Mandy was a trainer. She was behind the scenes,

was certainly watching the game, helping anyone who needed it. But she might have her cell.

She might be able to help me get a message to Axel.

She might be able to help me get Axel's head straight, to help me get the team back on track.

She might not pick up.

She—

"Fuck it."

I selected her contact, hit the button, and listened as the call rang through. Listened as it rang once, twice, three times. Then rang a fourth, sending my heart sinking. But even then, I planned my voicemail, was already drafting my follow-up text that I would send right after I hung up, when I heard, "Hello?"

For a second, I almost thought that it was my imagination, that I was hearing things in my mind.

Then I heard, "Bailey, hello? Are you okay?"

And I snapped up, sitting ramrod stiff. "Mandy."

She'd picked up.

She needed me to talk.

I needed to do it soon and—

"Bailey."

Sharper now. Calling me to focus.

"Mandy," I whispered. "Oh my God. I fucked up. I really, really fucked everything up."

"Breathe, honey. Tell me what's wrong."

So much.

So many stupid things.

"I need your help."

"I'm here."

She was, I knew she was.

So, I took a breath...and I told her everything.

And then Mandy and I came up with a plan.

Forty

I fumbled the pass and immediately was picked, my opponent snagging the puck, taking off for our zone, for Brit.

Creating another scoring opportunity.

We were already down two and didn't need to be digging out of an even bigger hole.

But if I didn't get my ass back, that was a real possibility.

I scrambled, fought to keep my edge, and then started skating back, closing in on the player, putting enough pressure on that Brit made the save, kicking the rebound out into the corner.

From there it was a fight to get it clear of our zone, to just survive the pressure from the other team long enough for us to get to the bench, to let someone else come on the ice and hopefully do something better than the shit I was shoveling out.

My lungs squeezed, air rushing out when I was checked into the boards.

Nothing I didn't deserve.

It was shit. The game was shit. *I* was shit.

But I managed to get the puck over the fucking blue line.

Then I hauled my ass to the bench.

I couldn't make eye contact with Calle, couldn't let myself see what was probably going to be disappointment in her eyes.

So, I just kept my gaze on my hands.

Get it together, Finnegan.

I was fucking trying. We were all out there. We were all scrabbling. We were all doing...well, not our best since we were fucking up left and right.

We were trying.

It just...wasn't good enough.

Not even close.

Don't think like that. Don't focus on the shit. Flush it down. Flush it away.

I was trying to flush. I was trying to let it all be washed down the drain.

But the goddamned drain was clogged. I needed a fucking plunger. I needed—

To get back on the ice.

So, I fucking got out there. I did it, and I kept stinking it up, kept fucking up. No matter how much flushing, how much I tried to compartmentalize my brain. No matter how much I tried to. Nothing helped.

But by some fucking miracle of miracles, we managed to hold them off to just that two goal lead.

No one, least of all me, was feeling good about it.

"Fucking hell," I muttered, tossing the water bottle back into the holder then standing, following the guys off the bench and down the hall, still trying to keep my gaze off Calle's, off Coach's. Definitely away from the cameras so on the off chance that they were on me, were streaming back home to our fans, to Bailey. Or, just as bad, onto the Jumbotron. I didn't want anyone here to see my despair.

We were going to lose this game.

I knew it.

My season was going to be over.

We weren't going to get Brit another Cup before she retired.

We were just going to lose, go home, and—

Someone grabbed my hand.

Blinking, I looked up, saw Mandy.

"Do I—" I started to ask if she needed me to step into the modified training suite they'd set up for the duration of the series.

But the look on her face had me shutting up.

I'd never understood the idiom of *ice in my veins*. Not until that moment. In that moment, when I saw Mandy's expression, I *knew* it. I *felt* it.

"What's the matter?" I rasped.

She tugged me into a room.

"What?"

She shoved a paper into my hands.

"*Mandy*, what's the matter?" I asked. "Is Bailey okay? Is—"

Her hands came to my shoulders, and she squeezed tightly enough that I froze, that any words in my mind fled.

"Read it," she ordered.

And then she was gone.

Then the door had closed behind her, the *click* of the latch sliding into the strike plate gunshot loud in the silent room.

It was loud enough to make me jump.

To crinkle the paper.

Read it.

It was just plain white computer paper, folded in half.

Heart pounding, I opened it up—

And then read the words scrawled on the inside.

FORTY-ONE

BAILEY

Mandy had helped me write the note.

She'd promised to get it to him as soon as possible.

I was glued to the television screen, watching the guys walk off the ice, and then trying to not pull my hair out as the commentators spent the next fifteen minutes talking about how the Gold were basically getting their asses handed to them.

Over and over.

Talking shit about my guys—and gal.

Were they playing their best? Fuck no.

But were they out of this?

Hopefully not.

Hopefully, not with the note.

Hopefully, it would help and not make things worse.

Hopefully, I wasn't so overconfident or delusional thinking it would settle Axel enough that he could work a miracle.

Because it was *all* I could do.

So, as they talked about my family being out of this, out of the series, out of the running for the Cup, I was shoveling cookies and popcorn into my mouth, and I was drinking a beer and I was hoping against hope that something might change.

Because I wasn't sure if I could forgive myself if I was the cause—

Which wasn't fair to me.

They were big boys. They were professionals.

They were tired and had injuries and were maybe ready for the season to be done.

Yes, they should be able to put it all aside and *play*.

But it was long, tough road.

And I'd made it tougher. On Axel. On the rest of them because they were a team and each piece in the team mattered.

Sighing, I stood up, shaking my arms, rolling my shoulders.

I needed to stop spinning on this roller coaster.

I needed to breathe and just take the outcome as it was.

I'd fucked up. I tried to fix it.

"Right, Bailey," I whispered. "You fucked up. You owned it. You tried to fix it." I let that sit for a minute, until I could almost believe it was true. "You *tried* to fix it. That's all you can do."

The commercials cut out and the game was back on, the players skating out on the ice, circling around, and lining up for the face-off, the rest loading up both benches, even as the commentators kept yapping about the slim chances the Gold had.

I plunked back onto the couch, clutched a pillow to my chest with one arm, my other going around Spock, fingers dipping into the soft black and white fur.

And I was breathing like I'd been sprinting around there on the ice, trying to keep up with those big behemoths of hockey players.

Both teams got settled. The goalies dealt with their creases, scraping their skates across them in the way they preferred, bunching snow up, shoving it in the goal, spreading it around the blue half circle. Then the doors were closed and the refs were in position and—

The puck was dropped.

It took exactly two seconds for me to see that there was a different team out on the ice.

There was a fire under the ass of every Gold player that hadn't been there last game, last period.

Hope blossomed anew.

My breathing steadied, or maybe I didn't breathe—didn't breathe as Josh scored about five minutes in, didn't breathe as Coop tapped one in a few minutes later, didn't breathe as Axel shoved the puck home with just thirty seconds left in the period.

Which, look, I got was actually impossible.

But it felt that way, felt like I hadn't moved an inch, hadn't breathed, hadn't blinked.

And anyway, that wasn't the point.

They were ahead, and—

I gasped.

Axel's face was on TV and as if he knew the camera was on him, he stared deep into the lens, as though he were looking at *me*.

Buttercup, he mouthed.

And every cell in my body relaxed.

He'd gotten the note.

He was telling me it was okay.

I *breathed*. For the first time in a period, I actually *breathed*.

And then I watched my man kill it on the ice.

———

They'd won.

I was bursting with excitement.

Because they'd *won!*

The game was more even in the third period, but the Gold had scored once more and Brit had made some really good saves that had helped keep them on top of the scoreboard.

And then the final buzzer had sounded, and it was like they'd already won the Cup.

They'd battled back.

They'd won decidedly.

They were back in the series.

I inhaled, eyes prickling, and began clearing the remnants of my snacks, doing my dishes, getting all my things ready for the morning.

The chores never stopped.

But that was okay.

Because I'd made it right—or I hoped so anyway.

I probably wouldn't be able to fully relax, not until I heard from him, not until we talked and—

Right.

Enough spinning.

I shoved my cell into my pocket and grabbed my jacket, shrugging into it as I stepped out onto the porch, Spock scooting out the opening and trailing behind me as I sat down on the porch steps and stared out into the late evening sky.

There was just a bit of light still present on the horizon, but the rest of the space overhead was navy, was twinkling with stars, draped with clouds.

I started to pull out my phone, but a noise drew my gaze to the road, and I watched as a sedan slowed.

The interior light was on.

I couldn't see the driver, just a silhouette.

A woman.

But just as I thought they might pull into my driveway, the car sped up, zipping down the road and disappearing around the corner.

Weird.

But maybe the woman had been lost. It was easy to get twisted up around here, to lose your way, especially when night had fallen.

Spock cuddled closer, and I leaned against the porch pillar, stroking my hand through his fur.

Not relaxed, necessarily, but content to wait for Axel to call, content to sit out here and just be for a few minutes after the stress I'd made out of my day.

A deep breath, releasing all that tension.

My eyes slid closed, and I just sat there in the quiet.

Spock whined.

"It'll be okay, bud," I murmured, scratching his ears.

I inhaled again, let it out.

And just sat.

Until...I caught a whiff of something in the air during one of my inhales.

It was...smoke?

My lids flew open, and I sucked in another breath, a deep one this time, and what hit my nostrils had me shooting to my feet, pulling in more air, trying to pinpoint the location, to smell for certain, to *know* for certain.

My gaze searching as I darted out toward the barn, spinning both ways, looking, *looking*—

And seeing...

An orange glow on the horizon.

Smoke in the air.

That orange glow.

A dry spring and—

Fire.

There was a fire on the hills.

And it was coming for the ranch.

FORTY-TWO

AXEL

The win tonight was...

Incredible.

It felt like we'd already won it all, that we'd crossed our biggest hurdle, could go home, and just cruise into the Cup.

I'd gotten it together.

We'd *all* gotten it together, had decided that we weren't ready for the season to be done.

So...we'd pushed on.

Scored some goals, got them on their back feet, and we'd won the *fucking game*.

Now we were giving the requisite interviews and I was hoping that Bailey had seen my homage into the camera, knew that I wasn't upset with her, not in the least.

It was okay.

And that she'd been worried enough to find a way to apologize to me mid-game, to let me know that she loved me, that we'd be okay...

That meant a lot.

It meant everything.

Love wasn't perfect, wasn't a smooth road without any bumps.

There were potholes and divergences and rumble strips and peeling paint.

But she'd tried to make it right, even despite the circumstances. Because she was worried that I was in my head and not playing well because of something she'd done.

She was right, of course.

I wasn't playing well.

And I'd been stuck in my own head.

But I was beating myself up, wasn't mad at her, not in the least.

I was desperate to get this shit over with, to get to a place where I could call her. Hell, I was desperate to call in a few favors and get her to San Francisco so she'd be in the stands when we won it all.

For the moment, though, I'd settle for a few quiet moments and a phone call.

Finally, the questions were done and the media gone, and I hit the showers, speeding through so I could get dressed, maybe find my way out to a quiet corner for that call.

But when I came out, rubbing a towel through my hair, the room had gone quiet.

Tense.

And my skin prickled, my stomach twisting, instincts instantly on full alert.

What the hell had happened?

I glanced around the room, but eyes didn't meet mine—gazes on their phones or their hands or their feet or...

Anywhere but mine.

Except Brit's.

She was sitting next to my spot.

Her cell was in her hand.

But her eyes, her eyes came to mine, held, and that ice settled into my veins all over again.

Only this time, I didn't think there was going to be a note

On numb ass legs, I walked over to her, sinking down onto the bench next to her, body still dripping with water, towel barely covering anything at all, and not giving one fuck that someone might walk in and see my balls.

Because the moment my ass hit the bench, Brit handed me her phone.

For a second, my eyes didn't register what I was seeing.

What I was reading.

Then it all hit at once.

I turned up the volume, listening to the local reporter talking about the fire that was burning up in the Sierra foothills.

For a moment, I hoped.

For a moment, I thought that because I'd finally dealt with my shit, gotten my life together, that for once, for *fucking* once, the universe wouldn't throw my life into a blender and hit the switch when I was happy.

That for once, I'd be able to *stay* happy.

Then I heard what had made everyone go so sober, so quiet.

"...the fire burned so hot and fast. It's being fueled by strong winds and unseasonably hot weather. CalFire and local departments are on scene, but the state of many of River's Bend's residents and buildings is unknown at this point. Evacuation orders have been issued for the entire county as the fire..."

I pulled out my phone.

I dialed Bailey.

The call wouldn't connect.

I texted, saw that she'd reached out earlier.

But that was before the game.

My text went through.

But there wasn't a reply.

And my calls, on the odd time they did connect, went straight to voicemail.

"The system is probably overwhelmed," Brit said softly.

"Yeah," I agreed.

But my stomach was in knots. I'd been down this road, had known better than to think I'd be able to have my happy ending.

Not *my* happy ending.

Not *my* life.

I was destined to have a glimpse of it, to have it just for a little bit...and then to lose it.

And I knew that wasn't just more bullshit, wasn't more spiraling in my fucked-up mind, because when Brit connected her phone to a local news station that was covering the fire, we all saw the banner at the bottom of the screen as the reporter talked—

River's Bend is on fire.

And I knew it wasn't a bullshit news story, trying to make something out of nothing.

Because I texted, I called, doing both over and over again.

And Bailey didn't answer *any* of them.

Not *one* time.

Instead, I got silence. I got calls that didn't connect. I got voicemail.

I got...worry.

And increasingly dire news reports.

———

Thank you for reading! I hope you loved meeting Axel and Bailey! The next book in the Rush Hockey trilogy is SO PUCKING OVER IT. **I had everything I had ever wanted... And it meant nothing...**

CLICK HERE TO READ SO PUCKING OVER IT NOW>

And if you enjoyed BIG PUCK ENERGY, you'll love the sexy,

sweet, and close-knit Breakers Hockey crew. The first book in the series, BROKEN, is now live!

It is sexy, hot, adorable and such a fun read. You will not be able to put this down!" —Amazon Reviewer

———

I so appreciate your help in spreading the word about my books, including sharing with friends! Please leave a review on your favorite book site!

You can also join my Facebook group, the Fabinators, for exclusive giveaways and sneak peeks of future books.

SIGN UP FOR ELISE FABER'S NEWSLETTER HERE: https://www.elisefaber.com/newsletter

Hate missing Elise's new releases? Love contests, exclusive excerpts and giveaways?

Then signup for Elise's newsletter here!

www.elisefaber.com/newsletter

And join Elise's fan group, the Fabinators (https://www.facebook.com/groups/fabinators) for insider information, sneak peaks at new releases, and fun freebies! Hope to see you there!

Rush Hockey

Big Puck Energy
Filthy Puckboy
So Pucking Over It

Also by Elise Faber

Billionaire's Club (all stand alone)

Bad Night Stand

Bad Breakup

Bad Husband

Bad Hookup

Bad Divorce

Bad Fiancé

Bad Boyfriend

Bad Blind Date

Bad Wedding

Bad Engagement

Bad Bridesmaid

Bad Swipe

Bad Girlfriend

Bad Best Friend

Bad Billionaire's Quickies

Gold Hockey (all stand alone)

Blocked

Backhand

Boarding

Benched

Breakaway

Breakout

Checked

Coasting

Centered

Charging

Caged

Crashed

A Gold Christmas

Cycled

Caught

Cap

Covered

Breakers Hockey (all stand alone)

Broken

Boldly

Breathless

Ballsy

Rush Hockey

Big Puck Energy

Filthy Puckboy

So Pucking Over It

Love, Action, Camera (all stand alone)

Dotted Line

Action Shot

Close-Up

End Scene

Meet Cute

Love After Midnight (all stand alone)

Rum And Notes

Virgin Daiquiri

On The Rocks

Sex On The Seats

Life Sucks Series (all stand alone)

Train Wreck

Hot Mess

Dumpster Fire

Clusterf*@k

FUBAR

Roosevelt Ranch Series (all stand alone, series complete)

Disaster at Roosevelt Ranch

Heartbreak at Roosevelt Ranch

Collision at Roosevelt Ranch

Regret at Roosevelt Ranch

Desire at Roosevelt Ranch

Phoenix Series (read in order)

Phoenix Rising

Dark Phoenix

Phoenix Freed

Phoenix: LexTal Chronicles (rereleasing soon, stand alone, Phoenix

world)

From Ashes

In Flames

To Smoke

KTS Series (all stand alone, series complete)

Riding The Edge

Crossing The Line

Leveling The Field

Scorching The Earth

Cocky Heroes World

Tattooed Troublemaker

About the Author

USA Today bestselling author, Elise Faber, loves chocolate, Star Wars, Harry Potter, and hockey (the order depending on the day and how well her team -- the Sharks! -- are playing). She and her husband also play as much hockey as they can squeeze into their schedules, so much so that their typical date night is spent on the ice. Elise is the mom to two exuberant boys and lives in Northern California. Connect with her in her Facebook group, the Fabinators or find more information about her books at www.elise-faber.com.

facebook.com/elisefaberauthor

amazon.com/author/elisefaber

bookbub.com/profile/elise-faber

instagram.com/elisefaber

tiktok.com/@elisefaberauthor

goodreads.com/elisefaber

www.ingramcontent.com/pod-product-compliance
Lightning Source LLC
Chambersburg PA
CBHW052043240626
47153CB00006B/2200